SURRENDER
TO THE
GENTLEMAN
PIRATE

BY HELEN LOUISE COX

Published in the United Kingdom by
Helen Cox Books.

Copyright © 2020 by Helen Louise Cox.

Ebook ISBN: 978-1-8380801-5-0
Paperback ISBN: 978-1-8380801-6-7
Hardback ISBN: 978-1-8380801-7-4

Other Romance Titles by Helen Louise Cox

Disarming the Wildest Warrior
Surrendering to the Gentleman Pirate
Swept Away by the Merman

Historical Notes

In my research, I have found no records of a Viscount of Pembroke or Earl of Wrexham. They are designed purely as fictional titles which reflect the peerage of the time. Bishop Richard Trevor did serve as the Bishop of St Davids at the time this book is set. His reaction to a band of pirates descending on a wedding he is officiating is, however, entirely imaginary.

There is a mention of dowries in this work even though the pirate captain hails from America. This wedding tradition was brought to the United States by European immigrants in the 17th Century.

1750

CHAPTER ONE

Bronwyn

Caged behind her dove-white veil, Bronwyn tried to steady her trembling hands. The shaking was so vigorous that petals from her bouquet of violets scattered to the floor like premature confetti. Most brides would interpret this as a portent of the happiness that awaited them on the other side of their wedding vows. To Bronwyn however, those falling petals were no more than a dark omen; a warning sign that there was no way out of this arrangement, no matter how much she might wish for one.

'Will you, Bronwyn Elin Rees, take this man as thy wedded husband?' said Bishop Trevor. 'Will you obey him, love him, and honour him, forsaking all others, so long as you both shall live?'

'I...' Bronwyn glanced over at her husband-to-be and heard her voice die away. With his jet-black hair and perfectly-tailored apparels, Leonard Price, Viscount of Pembroke, was a far more handsome suitor than a mottled old maid of twenty-nine had any right to hope for.

That is, if you favoured the quaffed, aristocratic look.

True, his turquoise eyes had, at times, a certain coolness to them that made Bronwyn want to reach for an extra shawl but she knew better than anyone that a person couldn't always help the way they looked. It was their kindness and virtue that mattered most and Mr Price had been nothing short of a gentleman throughout their brief courtship. Bronwyn held on to this thought as she tried, for second time, to answer Bishop Trevor's question.

'I... oh!'

Bronwyn's vow transformed into a shriek as a dagger whirled between she and her betrothed. The blade missed Bronwyn by less than an inch and she jumped as it tore Bishop Trevor's robe at the shoulder before sticking itself into the dark oak lectern, just behind where the minister was standing.

Bronwyn's eyes darted from the blade to Bishop Trevor's quivering finger as he pointed down the aisle of St Davids Cathedral, the colour draining from his usually rosy cheeks. 'Pirates!'

Whipping round, Bronwyn saw for herself that a band of rogues, twenty or so in number, had barged into the cathedral and were now advancing on the few guests attending her modest wedding service. Most of the men were broad in stature but the tallest seemed to be their leader. He strode towards them in a black shirt and breeches. He had a slightly rounded belly but was otherwise toned from the physical duties of life at sea. His long, sandy hair swished back and forth over his shoulders with every step.

The closer the bandits moved, the quicker friends and family members dispersed.

Considering every last one of the cutthroats wore leers laced with malice, Bronwyn couldn't much blame them for that. One of the rogues rounded on Leonard's father, the Earl of Wrexham. He had been unceasingly kind to her during her courtship with his son. Though he was unmistakably no-nonsense in his manner, he was frail in stature and Bronwyn did not like his chances of defending himself against these merciless marauders.

She squinted across at Mr Price as he edged behind one of the pews, trying to put a barrier between himself and the ever-nearing threat. His valet, Lothario Medlyn, who only ever left his liege's side when he slept, crossed his arms over his puffed-out chest and stood in front of his master. Medlyn was tall enough but not overly broad and thus unlikely to be any match for the advancing outlaws. Still, it seemed he was ready to defend his employer to the last, regardless.

'Mr Price, what'll we do?' Bronwyn hissed, masking her disappointment that his first thought was for his own safety, rather than hers or even his father's.

Before Bronwyn had her answer however, the tall man who she presumed to be the crew's captain bellowed in an accent that certainly wasn't local: 'She's the one we want!'

Bronwyn jumped as he pointed his long sword in her direction. 'Seize her!'

Seize *her*? Why? She had nothing to do with pirates.

Glancing over to a nearby corner, Bronwyn noticed her sister, Gwenllian cowering behind an arrangement of sea thrift. Likely the last of the pink blossoms St Davids would see for another year, now that April was almost over.

A low growl from an approaching brute re-established Bronwyn's attention on the peril at hand. It didn't matter much what became of her, so long as she kept her little sister safe. That was the promise she had made to her dying mother before she passed three months ago, and she intended to keep her word.

'Come 'ere now, lassie,' the brute said, baring an almost toothless grin. He grabbed Bronwyn's left wrist. Luckily, she led with her right and wasted no time in swinging her fist hard into her assailant's jaw, just as Alex had taught her to.

'If any rogue tries to take advantage, love, imagine we are separated by a thick, stone wall,' he had said, *'and that you must punch your way*

back to me. Hit as hard as you can Wynny, and don't stop until you are safe.'

As her knuckles connected with the man's jawbone, she tried not to think about how much more than stone separated her from her beloved Alexander now. Unlike the 'noble' Mr Price, he wouldn't have edged to the side lines. Alex would have given his last breath for her. In a way, she supposed, he had.

Utterly bewildered by Bronwyn's unexpected and repeated assault, the brute loosened his grip on her wrist just long enough for her to break free. Grabbing fistfuls of her silk wedding gown to avoid what would surely be a deadly fall if she faltered, Bronwyn dashed for all she was worth towards the side entrance of the cathedral. Once outside, she would be able to raise the alarm, save everyone from these bandits and, after his pathetic display of cowardice, call off her engagement to Mr Price. She had long wanted a valid reason to reject his offer of marriage, and now she had one. She was just about to twist the door handle when two strong arms clinched around her and lifted her clean off the ground.

'Let me go!' Bronwyn screamed, while kicking and bucking and twisting her way out of the unrelenting embrace. In her fight to get away she had turned herself about enough to see it was the captain who held her. 'Let me go or suffer the consequences,' she snapped at him.

The captain let out a rich, deep laugh. 'I think not, my pretty.'

The pirate's mirth only renewed Bronwyn's determination to get away. Again, she kicked and scratched and writhed, and in the struggle her veil was knocked to the stone floor, revealing the full terror that lay beneath.

Bronwyn had to give the pirate his due, he managed to fight a look of disgust as his brown eyes, which burned like amber in the afternoon sunlight streaming through the cathedral windows, examined the marks and scars that marred most of her face on the left side.

He did not loosen his grip or jump back in shock. This, Bronwyn admitted privately, was a pity as it would have given her the advantage, and a means of escape.

As he frowned at her, in a way one might find disconcerting, it seemed he was gripped more by fascination than fear. Perhaps he was trying to imagine how beautiful she would be if the left side of her face matched the right, which was an untouched canvas of smooth, pale skin.

Bronwyn was aware of various scuffles playing out around them but as the pirate examined her, and she studied him in turn, the noise seemed to fade away until the world fell quiet. Just long enough for her to notice that he was not without scars himself, though the dark, red line that ran across his lips was hardly a patch on her own afflictions. Despite this obvious blemish, there looked to be a softness to those lips. And in dwelling on that thought, the tiny hairs on the back of her arms stood to attention.

'What's the matter, pirate?' Bronwyn said, shaking herself out of her prior enchantment. 'Trying to think of a more appropriate pet name for me than "my pretty?" Ask enough people in the village and I'm sure they'll provide you with one.' In a bid to seem braver than she truly felt, she moved her face closer to his. As she did so, she could smell the salt of the ocean on him and the sweetness of molasses which, she wagered, was a strong indication of just how much rum the man drank. As she spoke her next words, Bronwyn lowered her voice almost to a hiss.

'Some people call me a witch, you know, and say that these scars are the mark of the devil.'

Those eyes of amber considered her for a moment, and then the pirate laughed again. 'I'm already too far gone to worry about consorting with devils, my lady.'

Without another word, the pirate turned Bronwyn to face her groom while holding his sword to her throat. The metal was cold against her skin and was pressed firmly enough to her neck that she was certain any more struggling would draw blood.

'Everybody cease!' the pirate bellowed. 'Unless you wish this lady dead.'

The other thugs obeyed the command of their captain while the wedding guests, at the threat to Bronwyn's life, halted their defensive movements.

'W-w-what do you want?' Price stammered out.

'I want you to pay your penance for past sins, you blubbering hog.'

Bronwyn felt the pirate's grip on her tighten as he said this. What on earth had Mr Price done to inspire such fury and outrageous public insult?

'Pay? What?'

'Come on, Leo. Don't pretend. You *must* recognise me?'

Price stared harder at the pirate and then withdrew a step, his eyes widening. 'Miles? Is that you?'

'That's Captain Miles Nash now, Leo. And as to what I want, it comes to this: I am stealing your beloved away for thirty days. Fear not, I will return her, which is more kindness than you ever paid me. Thirty days is more than enough time for you to gather the assortment of fine jewellery your mother left you when she died. Including her prized ruby necklace – The Eye of the Sun.'

Bronwyn suppressed a sigh. So the pirate was after Mr Price's riches and she, it seemed, was to be a bargaining chip. She should have guessed it would come down to something as callous as that. Although… he had said something about past sins, and indicated some former cruelty from Price. If all the pirate really wanted was riches he could accrue such plunder without sailing into port. No, whatever his reasons, this pirate wanted more than just gold. From the sounds of things he was thirsty for revenge. Either way, if the pirate did steal her away to his ship for thirty days her reputation would never recover. But then, perhaps with Alex gone that didn't matter so much anymore. It's not as if she would ever love like that again.

'How - how do you know about my mother's ruby?' said Price, his tone turning from fear to mild indignation. 'That gem has been a family heirloom for generations. Nobody has ever spoken about –'

'What I know, and how I came by the information, is not your concern. Here is what *you* need to know: if anyone follows us to our ship, your lady's throat will be cut and she will bleed to death, slowly on the sands. If you fail to deliver your treasured jewels to me when I return in thirty days, she will suffer the same fate and we will torch every village along the coast of Pembroke. You will then be known as the Viscount who let his county burn.'

'But, but, but –' Price began.

'You have thirty days, Price, do not disappoint me,' Nash growled over his shoulder as he dragged Bronwyn out of the church, his blade never once leaving her jugular.

CHAPTER TWO

Miles

She was doing her best to hide it, but Miles could see his hostage was shaking as his first mate, Rookwood hustled her into the small, wooden cabin that comprised his quarters. His ship, The Serpent was a decent-size for a galleon so journeys were relatively smooth but she looked so unsteady on her feet that he rose to help her into the chair at the other end of the dining table.

'Unhand me, pirate,' Bronwyn almost spat as she eased herself into a sitting position.

With some reluctance, Miles released her forearm, so soft to the touch and part obscured by the delicate silk sleeve of her wedding gown. Somewhere, deep inside, disgust erupted at the thought that the only reaction he inspired in a lady these days was revulsion. And what else could he expect, when he had dragged her all the way back to his ship with a sword at her throat? No self-respecting woman would give a man who did that the benefit of the doubt, nor should she.

He watched over her as she closed her eyes and breathed deeply, seemingly trying to get a hold of her senses.

'I am sorry, my lady, sea-sickness is a terrible thing.'

'I do not suffer from sea-sickness, Captain Nash,' she snapped. 'At least not as you know it... oh!'

Her eyes sprang open and she looked down to her side. Leaning over the table Miles saw that Dodger, his Newfoundland dog, was merrily licking Bronwyn's hand.

'Hello there,' she said, her voice, with that strange, alluring lilt the Welsh were known for, was so much gentler than when it had been when she had addressed him.

That mangy cur needed no other invitation to jump up and place his front paws on Bronwyn's lap so she might more easily rub his dark brown ears. And so he might look with longing eyes at the meats spread out on the table.

'Oh, you poor little fella,' Bronwyn said.

'Don't be fooled. That dog eats better than me,' Miles said. 'Dodger, down, down I said!'

'Don't shout at a defenceless creature,' Bronwyn scolded him before turning back to the dog. 'Stuck on a pirate ship with an American as your captain. What a terrible life, eh old boy?'

Dodger, the treacherous beast, made a growling noise as though agreeing with Bronwyn's statement.

'Had I known you were so soft at heart for flea-bitten mutts, I'd have brought the hound to the cathedral and used him to lure you to the ship.'

Bronwyn looked deep into Dodger's eyes, while scratching the back of his neck. 'I may well have followed you. Dogs don't care how much money you have or what you look like. Treat them well and you'll never know a purer love…' she seemed to catch herself then, making conversation with a pirate, and trailed off.

As she heaped yet more adoring fuss on the animal, Miles took the opportunity to consider her. By candlelight, her scars were much reduced but there was still no ignoring the way they dominated what would have otherwise been a perfect face. The marks looked like burns. What had caused them? And what was a man like Price doing marrying a woman with such afflictions? He had no compassion, no finer feelings. He was selfish and superficial. The only conclusion Miles had been able to draw was that the poor woman had some fortune to steal, just like his darling Cecily had. He couldn't help but feel pity for the lady. Being caught between himself and Price just now was not a fortunate predicament for any soul.

If there had been a more straightforward way of having his revenge on Price for the suffering he had caused, Miles would have taken it. But circumstances were such that abducting his betrothed was the only fitting punishment. That said, he bore her no ill will for her poor taste in suitors and wanted the next thirty days to pass as easily as possible. Thus, he had ordered the cook to lay out the best of what food they had. In his experience, people were more amicable on a full stomach or perhaps, he considered rubbing his amble gut, that was just him.

'Leave the dog now,' he said gesturing to the spread cook had laid out for them, 'and eat.'

The lady eased the dog off her lap and at once seemed to regain some of the pluck she'd shown back in St Davids. Miles fought a smile, still not quite believing that he had watched her punch his quarter master, Roberts, several times. It was then that he noticed the lady raising an eyebrow at him and tightening her mouth in a manner that spoke of pure resolve.

'Eat,' he said again, more firmly this time.

'No.'

'No?'

'I've lost my appetite,' Bronwyn said.

'Because of the company or the food?'

He watched as Bronwyn took her time eyeing the last of the fresh cut meats they had on board, and the vegetables the ship's cook had taken pains to season to the best of his limited abilities.

'Both,' she shot back at him once her assessment of the table was complete.

Miles frowned. What? Was the best they had to offer not good enough for the bride of Leonard Price? The thought of all this food going to waste because she felt like being obstinate at once aroused his temper.

'It was not a request, *Princess*, it was an order.'

'I don't take orders from you, or anyone else.'

'You are, may I say, speaking rather boldly for a woman who is at the mercy of a band of ruthless pirates.'

Bronwyn shrugged. 'It's of little consequence, Leonard will find a way of rescuing me long before the thirty days are up.'

'You have such faith in your gallant groom.'

'I have faith that he will not want to hand over his family heirlooms for a woman such as I so yes, he will probably make some other plan to come for me. If you weren't so half-witted you'd have understood that a face like this wasn't a fair trade for any number of precious jewels in the first place. Still, in the vain hope that Leonard will pay up, I'm betting you'll do all you can to keep your cargo intact. And if I were you, I would keep that thought keenly at the front of your mind. If my betrothed does choose to trade, and one of your greasy apes has so much as laid a hand on me, I'll be certain to tell Leonard not to hand you even a piece of gold in exchange for spoiled goods.'

'How will you tell him you're spoiled goods if we cut out your tongue?' Miles was fairly sure he'd done a decent job of making this seem like a real possibility. He didn't want to hurt the woman but he had to command her respect if his plan was to work. 'I know Price of old, he is not a good listener and may even thank me for ridding you of that particular appendage.'

A low growl came from the corner where Dodger now lay.

That insolent canine! Weren't dogs supposed to be loyal to their masters?

Bronwyn smirked, at seemingly having won the dog's immediate allegiance. 'Off the top of my head I should imagine I could put such a message in writing. And if you believe, Captain Nash, that my future husband would not miss my tongue then you vastly underestimate what I can do with it.'

Miles noticed Bronwyn's blue eyes widen for a second as she realised what she had just said but then she narrowed them again and folded her arms. As if to pretend it had been her intention all along to speak in such a forward manner.

At her words, a diverting image formed in his mind of Bronwyn kneeling at his feet. Her mouth open wide, impatient for a taste of him. He pushed the image from his mind. He must not get distracted. He was supposed to be a seasoned, sea-hardy pirate. And in most ways he was. Except for *that* way. Though he had lived thirty years, his experience with women had been voluntarily limited. He had vowed not to touch another woman until he had avenged Cecily. Carnal matters had not interested nor concerned him that much of late... until now.

'If you refuse to eat,' he said, trying to think of something – anything – else than what talents Bronwyn might have with her tongue, 'then you will be sent back to your room with nothing.'

'Room?' Bronwyn scoffed. 'Prison cell, you mean.'

'If you'd ever spent time in a prison cell, you'd make no such comparison,' Miles said, keeping his voice low, dangerous.

'Send me away with no food if you wish, I'd rather keep my own company than be here with you.'

Scowling, Miles stalked to the door. 'Rookwood!' he barked, attracting the attention of his first mate. Rookwood was the only one on the ship besides himself he would trust to chaperone the lady; he dare not contemplate what the rest of his crew might do with Bronwyn if they got hold of her. He may have kidnapped her to spite Price but he wasn't going to see her defiled, not on his ship.

'Aye, Captain?' Rookwood said, raising his bushy eyebrows in expectation.

'Escort the future Mrs Price back to her room and ensure you lock the door and return the key to me at once. And while you're at it, find her something other to wear than that tattered wedding gown. We should have something amongst the loot.' With a bit of luck, Rookwood would interpret this request as opportunistic lechery; that a pirate captain would want any female captive to look as presentable for him as possible. In truth, the sheer number of tears in Bronwyn's wedding gown were revealing far more of her soft skin than he could bear to look at. A rip along the left side of her dress revealed the beguiling inward jut of her waist and he couldn't afford to indulge such distractions.

Rookwood nodded. 'Aye, Captain.'

Bronwyn stood from her seat at the table and walked shakily to the door.

Miles's first instinct was to reach out and steady her but he stopped himself. 'Don't expect to be offered food like this again, *Princess*. It will be water and sea biscuits for the next thirty days, if you're lucky.'

Bronwyn didn't respond, at least not verbally. She merely shot him a glare that cut him almost as deep as a dagger might and then followed Rookwood to the room next to his cabin. Miles had decided to hold her in there so that he could keep a close watch on the wench and foil any escape attempts. Especially important after any hope of winning her compliance with a decent meal had been dashed.

Closing the door, Miles sighed and sat down at the table.

He patted his knee and summoned Dodger but the dog didn't move. He merely looked at Miles with those large, sorrowful eyes that had prompted the pirate to take the dog in when he'd found him wandering the docks in New York.

'Do not look at me that way, you hound,' Miles said. The dog whined and Miles admitted that he felt the mutt's pain.

If Bronwyn insisted on being this uncooperative, it was going to be a long thirty days.

CHAPTER THREE

omewhere, in the far distance, Bronwyn heard a woman screaming. For a moment, those desperate shrieks were the only thing she could sense through the cloying darkness. Until she caught the faint scent of molasses on the air, and the salt of the ocean. It was only when Bronwyn felt two firm hands grip her shoulders however, that she roused enough to understand the screams she had heard were her own.

Her eyes jolted open and met a set of deep brown eyes, the amber in them just visible thanks to a candle burning, somewhere. The captain sat at the edge of her cot. His frown deep. His sandy hair falling in soft waves. She felt her face crumple, and tears burn their way out as she realised she had been dreaming. Or, more accurately, had been caught in a nightmare. Her lost Alex had been drowning and she couldn't save him.

'Easy now,' Nash said, as she wept harder than she had in a very long time while all the while hating herself for showing any sign of weakness in front of her captor.

The captain held her steady and hesitated just for a moment before sweeping a strand of hair from her brow. He grazed her cheek with the back of his hand and the warmth of his skin against hers was more of a comfort that she'd care to admit.

She scowled at the effect he seemed to have on her. How she despised this man. For kidnapping her. For stealing her away onto this ship and dredging up memories she'd worked hard to forget. But she hated herself more as her stare fixed once again on the captain's lips, surrounded by stubble. As she noticed how close they were and how easy it would be to lean forward and kiss him. She dismissed the feelings as an unfortunate side-effect of the unrelenting fear she felt at being at the mercy of the ocean and a band of outlaws, no doubt just as cruel. Yes, this, alongside the manner in which she had been so suddenly starved of affection with Alex's passing three years ago, is what made her eyes wander to the scarred mouth of a violent stranger.

For his part, the captian wore a strange expression that Bronwyn found difficult to read. It seemed to her like a mixture of pity and lust. She admitted privately that she was as guilty as he when it came to the lust part. But she wouldn't have him thinking of her as a poor, scarred little thing, desperate for sympathy.

With some effort she pulled herself away. 'Leave me,' she said, turning her back on him.

She heard the sound of wood scraping as the captain pulled up a chair.

'I would gladly respect your request,' said Nash, his voice gentle. 'But I can't have you screaming out in the middle of the night and waking the crew. Once I'm assured you'll sleep soundly, I'll take my leave.'

Bronwyn narrowed her eyes. The captain's room was just next door so he could just as easily rush to her side from there if it was truly the racket that concerned him. No, one of two things was happening here. Either the pirate wanted her to fall asleep so he could take advantage without her knowledge or he was using his captainly duties to mask a kindness he was paying her. Sitting by her side, keeping her company until she fell asleep. Pirate captains weren't exactly renowned for their kindness to their female captives but after the little chat she and Nash had had earlier about spoiled goods, she doubted it was the former.

In recalling their earlier conversation, Bronwyn felt her cheeks burn and thanked God she was turned away from the pirate so he could not see her blushing. What in the name of all the saints had prompted her to let on she had sultry ways with her tongue?

It was true, of course.

Alex had taught her how to gratify him that way and she had instructed him on finding the perfect point of pleasure between her own thighs, but this was not the kind of information one relayed to a stranger, let alone a swashbuckling bandit.

'Who is Alex?' Nash asked. Bronwyn started at this question. She must have called Alex's name during her terror. Nash seemed to be taking pains to keep his tone tender, but she was not appeased. The mere sound of her lost love's name on the lips of a pirate sent her into a fury.

She reeled to face Nash so he might understand she was not to be trifled with on this matter.

'Don't you dare speak his name,' she said. 'Don't you ever speak his name again. You don't deserve to... I barely deserve to.'

Tears threatened once again but Bronwyn swallowed them back, determined not to give the pirate the satisfaction of breaking down for a second time in his presence.

'He must be a good man for you to react so,' Nash said.

'He was,' Bronwyn snapped back. 'Better than any I have known, or any I ever will.'

'I take, by your use of the past tense, that he is no longer with you. If this is the case, I am sorry. I... know how it feels to lose a person you truly love.'

She swallowed hard and lowered her eyes. 'Do not feed me lies, pirate.'

'Be warned, I do not respond well to being called a liar, lady,' said Nash in a voice so low and deadly for a moment she wondered if he might strike her for the insult.

When he remained still she pressed him further. 'You expect me to believe that a man such as you knows what it is to love and lose that way?'

'Whether you believe it is really of no concern to me. When it feels as though there is a hole in your heart, that will never, ever heal, what does it matter what anyone believes of you?'

Bronwyn studied Nash's face looking for a smirk that might suggest he was taunting her but she could find none. He stared off in the distance, as though caught in a trance, embroiled in some fancy. His words echoed exactly how she would have described the pain of losing Alex, if asked. But was a man like him really capable of loving another as she had loved her Alexander?

After a moment he snapped out of his daydream and slowly turned those eyes of amber on her. 'Does it hurt or help to speak of him, the one you lost?'

'Both,' she said, grateful that Nash was at least honouring her request to not use Alex's name. An image of her lost love's cheeky grin formed in her mind. A memory that always came with a slight sting. On picturing his face, she couldn't resist speaking of his beauty out loud. 'He was the most perfectly handsome man I have ever known. All of the young girls in the village thought so too. He could have had any one of them but he picked me, he loved this face when almost nobody else could. A young man with every woman falling at his feet, and he chose me.'

'He sounds wise, as well as kind,' said Nash. 'It is clear to anyone with a brain, besides your poor choice in grooms, that you are a good woman.'

Again, Bronwyn was sure the pirate must be mocking her but when she looked at his face she could see his expression was earnest, sincere. Why was he being so cordial when just a few hours ago he had a sword to her throat and after that had sentenced her to thirty days of water and sea biscuits? Was there some part of him that felt guilty? That wanted redemption? If there was, she wouldn't be the one to grant it to him that was for sure. Due to her scars, Bronwyn was used to poorer treatment than most but she drew the line at forgiving a man who had kidnapped her, regardless of what the good book said.

'When you look as I do, people are not quick to see the finer qualities in you,' she continued to muse out loud, remembering her Alex. If she thought hard enough about him, she might forget she was trapped on a ship that sailed the very ocean that had claimed his life.

'I am sorry to hear your afflictions have caused people to shy from you. When truly it is not your face at all but the sharpness of your tongue they should fear.'

Bronwyn looked harder at Nash in the dim candlelight and saw the smirk she had been expecting all along, playing over those lips that seemed to so often catch her attention. 'Oooh,' she said. 'I'm not sure you get to tease me so on the same day that you kidnap me.'

'Fear not, it is after midnight,' Nash said. His tone earnest even though the grin on his lips had widened.

Though she fought it as hard as she could, Bronwyn almost smiled at his quip. 'You needn't think your cruelty is forgiven just because you have a knack for comedy, captain.'

The smile fell from Nash's face. 'I wouldn't expect it.'

'Good. I am glad we understand one another.'

A silence fell between the pair and Bronwyn guessed what the captain might be pondering. The same thing almost everyone pondered once they found an easy rhythm of conversation with her.

'Would it be rude to ask what happened to cause those scars?'

'Frightfully,' said Bronwyn. 'But you're a pirate and thus can be forgiven for not knowing any better.'

Nash didn't respond to her jibe but waited patiently for her to speak again.

'When I was nine years old someone forgot to put the last candle out before we all went to sleep. The flame caught the curtains and the whole house went up. Luckily I started and raised the alarm. I thought my little sister Gwenllian was behind me as I fled the house but when I looked back I could see she was still trapped inside,' at the mention of her sister's name, Bronwyn thought she might cry again. She could only hope that she was safe back in Pembroke and none of the crew had taken their chance to corrupt or wound her during their attack on the cathedral. 'My parents were both ill, and not very able so I ran back in and, as far as possible, used myself as a shield against the flames so she would be kept safe. She has a burn mark on her left leg but I took the brunt of it.'

When Bronwyn finished speaking Nash was silent for a good long while. When he did speak, his voice was even gentler than it had been when he had spoken of Alex. 'You were a very brave little girl. And it doesn't take a pirate captain to see that you have grown into a very brave woman. Hear me now, I need to keep you on this ship for thirty days. I would not do it if there was another way, but there is none. After what you have shared with me I promise, however, that your days here will be as free of hardship as possible.'

'Why? Why do you *need* to do this?'

Nash leaned forward in his chair, and after a moment's pause, stroked her hair. To her surprise, she let him, without comment or rebuttal. 'Ask me tomorrow. It is not a good idea to speak of such things before sleep.'

'But I'm not tired,' Bronwyn said, though even as she did so, a yawn escaped her lips. 'Oh... all right, perhaps I'm more weary than I realised.'

'Get some rest. I will watch over you until you are asleep.'

Bronwyn's first instinct was to tell him he should do no such thing. But something about the idea of Nash watching over her while she slept did make her feel safe. As her eyes grew heavy, she told herself that she felt this way because no matter what, Nash needed her alive and unharmed. He clearly knew how to use a sword in a crisis and would defend his cargo against any threats. Yes, that must be why she felt safe in the company of a pirate.

CHAPTER FOUR

'Mast ahoy!'

Miles's eyes sprang open at the call from the crow's nest out on deck. He almost groaned with frustration but managed to stay quiet. He lay in Bronwyn's cot. Her head rested on his chest and all he could smell was her delicious scent, akin to the smell of ripe grapefruit.

What he would give to go on lying here, holding her in his arms, feeling her body rest against his in what seemed to be sheer contentment. Yes, his rod had strained against his breeches for much of the night and on odd occasions when she had tossed or turned she had rubbed against him in a manner that had made his hips gently thrust in her direction. He thought once or twice that the proximity of this beguiling maiden would drive him mad and yet he had found himself more than willing to slip deeper into insanity.

If another ship was approaching theirs, however, he could not risk laying here a moment longer.

Slowly and gently, he eased Bronwyn back into the cot and slid out. For a moment she seemed to stir and he feared he had woken her but then just as quickly, she turned over, pulling the blankets with her.

He sighed in relief.

He had stayed at her side much longer than he had meant to the night before. He could not take his eyes off her face as she slept. Nor take his mind off the story she had told about saving her sister from the fire. When she had shared that with him, he had needed every ounce of strength not to take her in his arms and kiss every scar on that perfectly imperfect face. To show her that to him, those scars were just as beautiful, if not more so, than the part that remained untouched by the fire.

Before he'd had anywhere close to his fill of looking at her, she began to shiver with incredible might and, though he knew it was a liberty, he had moved closer and wrapped his arms around her, persuading himself it was to provide warmth. Her shivering had stopped at once, and she had embraced him in return, pulling him into the cot seemingly without any sense of what she was doing.

He had meant to disentangle himself, truly. That was the noble thing to do after all. But nobody had ever really held him this way and thus he found himself unable to resist. In the cold light of day however, Miles realised how lucky it was he had awoken first. Though in his fancies she would welcome the sight of him in her bed, come morning light, given her obvious disdain for him, the reality of such a situation would be somewhat different. He did not wish to cause her any more distress than he had already. Of course if she had been some cold-hearted, entitled wench, the kind he had imagined Price finally settling down with, he wouldn't have had to grapple with such crises.

Running his hands through his hair, Miles stepped out onto the deck. The crew were already busy with their morning chores; nets were being mended; rigging and knots being inspected and, given the call from their young look-out, Jimmy, all canons were being checked for powder. Miles marched over to Rookwood who was looking across the Atlantic to the west through his spyglass.

'Predator or prey?' Miles asked.

'Looks to be a smaller ship than ours. I would have to say, prey,' said Rookwood.

Miles rubbed a hand over his stubble, which had grown long enough overnight to be soft to the touch. 'Within the month, we'll have enough treasure out of Price for everyone on this ship to retire. We'll not risk confrontation with the lady on board. If something goes wrong and they steal her from us, we'll have no leverage to make Price pay up.'

Rookwood fixed his pale grey eyes on Miles and seemed to weigh up his argument. 'We'll steer around her then?'

'Aye.' Miles was about to add something more when the sound of a man screaming echoed from one of the cabins. Not just one of the cabins, from Bronwyn's cabin.

Miles's heart stopped for a moment as he realised he hadn't locked her door. Cursing under his breath, he rushed back across the deck, Rookwood following closely behind.

Bursting into Bronwyn's cabin, Miles was met with a sight that at once turned his blood to lava.

Bronwyn stood pale and shaking against the wall while Roberts knelt on the floor groaning and clutching at his right arm.

'What is happening in here?' Miles growled.

Roberts held up his hand. A knife had been pushed straight through it. Blood-was spattered everywhere. 'The wench stole the knife from my belt and stabbed me,' Roberts wailed.

'If Mr Roberts does not wish to be stabbed, he should not touch ladies without their permission,' Bronwyn said.

Before Miles realised what he was doing he had Roberts by the scruff of the neck and pinned against the nearest wall. 'How dare you touch her?' he boomed in Roberts's bewildered face.

'She's just a scarred little thing, Cap'n. I didn't think you'd want her and I didn't think it'd matter if we 'elped ourselves as long as we gave her back when the thirty days were up.'

Miles squeezed Roberts's neck harder. 'You think Leonard Price will trade his jewels for a woman who has been defiled by pirates?' he seethed. There was no point in arguing with Roberts about the breach of decency. A bitter old sea dog like Roberts would see no wrong in touching a woman however he so chose. 'Give me one good reason why I shouldn't throw you overboard?' Miles spat.

'Come on now, Captain,' Roberts croaked out. 'I'm the one who 'elped you build this crew. I 'ad all the contacts, didn't I? Without me you wouldn't have 'ad a hope in 'ell of getting at Price.'

'This is the last time that favour will save you, Roberts,' Miles bit out, loosening his grip just enough for Roberts to catch his breath. 'If I catch you even looking at Br– our captive at any point in the next twenty-nine days, I'll happily make shark food out of you. Understood?'

'Understood, Cap'n,' Roberts said, gasping.

Slowly, Miles released the thug who shot a disgruntled grimace at Bronwyn before slinking off to tend to his hand. A few moments later Dodger came rushing in, barking at the top of his voice.

'It's no point raising the alarm now, mutt,' Miles said to the dog. 'The peril is past.'

Brightening at once at the sight of the somewhat useless canine, Bronwyn chuckled as he jumped up to lick the side of her face. She then followed him up onto the deck as he tore off, barking like the mad dog he was. Miles hadn't planned on letting her roam free around the deck but he hadn't planned on kidnapping a genuinely wholesome woman either. He suspected she was likely in need of some fresh air after the frightful awakening she'd had at the hands of Roberts and thus did not stop her.

'Are you hurt, my lady?' Miles asked, approaching her while she stood at the ship's edge, looking over the Atlantic, with Dodger jumping and yipping around her.

'Fear not, Captain,' she said, her tone arid. 'Your cargo is still intact.'

'That is… not why I was asking.'

'Really? You don't honestly expect me to believe this gentleman pirate act, do you?'

'Act?'

'You may have disarmed me last night when I was weary and homesick, Captain, but I am not a fool who can be so easily pacified. When it comes down to it, this is kidnap and you are nothing but a common thief.'

She raised a single eyebrow before walking away from him. Miles turned to watch her depart, desperately trying to think of something to say in return. Before he could find any words however, Rookwood bellowed: 'Attack, attack! Take cover!'

A bullet flew between Miles and Bronwyn. He stared in the direction of fire to see a ship closing on them fast, the ship that they had taken pains to avoid. Several crew members stood on the edge of the vessel, pistols in hand. One of them was aiming at Bronwyn. She turned, confused by the sudden clamour. Knowing that if he didn't act that instant, the lady would be hit, Miles managed to leap and knock her down to the deck just in time while bullets flew over their heads.

When he landed on top of her, he almost cried out in lustful agony as his body pushed hard into hers. It gave him more than a hint about how perfectly her little body would fit into his if the opportunity ever arose. The blush in her cheeks suggested she didn't exactly loathe the feeling of his body pushed so hard against her but, given her prior accusation that the kindnesses he paid her were pretence, he doubted she would ever admit an attraction to him, even if she harboured one.

All chaos was breaking out around them as he stared down into her eyes, which were bluer than any ocean he had sailed. He should be pitching in, protecting his men and yet he could not tear his gaze from her. Almost against his will, he felt his mouth ever so slowly drift closer to hers. Oh, how perfect it would be to kiss her, just once. Then, perhaps, he could get his mind back on his original mission. She stared up at him, panting almost as hard as he was as he leaned into her. He waited for her to push him away but she made no move to. Their lips couldn't have been more than a whisker apart when Rookwood shouted. 'All hands on the cannons!'

A command that should have come from Miles. But instead he was preoccupied with this woman who was supposed to be nothing more to him than a token to barter with. Scowling, he hoisted himself up and then pulled Bronwyn to her feet, shielding her with his body as he hurried her back to her cabin.

Gripping her wrist a little tighter than he would like to convey the urgency of the matter, he sat her down in the chair next to her cot. 'Stay in here and don't make a sound. If we are boarded and the enemy realises you are in here, they might guess I have the only key to this door. And if they get in they will not treat you as kindly as I have, do you hear me?'

'Whatever you say, Captain,' Bronwyn almost sneered at him. 'Dodger will keep me company, won't you boy?'

Dodger nuzzled himself into Bronwyn's body.

Miles released her wrist, watching on as she wrapped her arms around the cur. Trying to ignore the fact that at that moment he envied his own dog, he slammed the door to her cabin shut and locked it tight. He stepped back into the fray, the smell of gunpowder filling his lungs; the shouts and wails of the crew filling his ears. He cursed under his breath. It seemed he was ever doomed to be drawn into fights that he did not start and, if that were the case, he couldn't help but wonder the long-term price he would pay.

CHAPTER FIVE

In spite of herself, Bronwyn sighed in relief when the door to her cabin flew open and Nash stumbled through the frame. She had no sense of how long she had listened to agonizing groans and pistol fire but it had felt like days. Her relief soon turned to dread however, when she noticed the front of the captain's black shirt was wet. Not with sea water, but, given the red smears across his hands, with blood. 'What have you done to yourself?' Bronwyn scorned, instinctively helping Nash into a chair. Then she rushed over to a pitcher of water that had been rather thoughtfully left for her to wash with.

'Let me see,' she said, kneeling at his feet. The blood seemed to come from below the left side of his stomach.

'I do not need medical attention, woman,' Nash said through gritted teeth, pressing a hand into his wound. 'I came only to check that the enemy had not somehow got to you.'

'I see, you'd rather bleed to death than let me look at it, would you?'

'Maybe I would,' he said, with such stubbornness that Bronwyn might have been amused had she not been distracted by the pool of dark liquid she could see swelling around his hand.

'Miles,' she said softly. The sound of his first name seemed to startle him. Or was it because of the tone she had used? After half-understanding, through the bleary haze of sleep, that she was pulling the pirate into her cot last night, she had felt the need to be stern with him this morning. His body heat had been irresistible armour against the cold but she did not want him to get the wrong idea. Of course, now he was behaving doggedly due to her earlier attitude, but she wasn't about to have his death on her conscience. 'Please, let me see.'

After another few moments of hesitation, Nash slowly lifted his shirt just far enough for her to see the knife wound.

She frowned. 'This looks quite deep. I'm no doctor but from what I've seen of such things it's probably best if I at least wash it.'

'Why?' he said. 'Why do you care if I'm injured? Why would you care if I die… when I don't?'

Though she did her best not to show it, his words surprised Bronwyn. Up until now the captain had shown no signs that he was unhappy enough with his lot to want to die. Where had this sudden wish for an end come from?

'Because if you die, Mr Roberts will have no hands left by the end of the voyage – and from the looks they've been giving me, neither will most of the crew. And who knows if I'll be able to stop every hand that reaches for me if you're not around to protect my honour.' Bronwyn smiled as she said this, pleased that she had come up with a legitimate excuse to help this man. Her explanation was true enough but it was also true that being locked in this room while a battle raged outside had given her time to think about what she had said to Nash on the deck earlier. In particular, she was concerned that they may have been the last words she ever said to him. She didn't understand why that should concern her, given that he had kidnapped her against her will. But something about him dying, right after she had been so cold towards him, made her stomach churn.

'I am sure you could find a more noble protector. You deserve such a one.' Bronwyn broadened her smile but did not dare make eye contact with the captain. This was not the first time he had made such a comment. Things that indicated affection and respect for her. And if she were to look into his eyes of amber when he passed such observations, she may forget that he had made her his captive.

Just like she had last night.

Oh Heavens, she might deny it to him if he ever questioned her about it but there was little point in denying it to herself any longer. He had tried to warm her and she, a girl so starved of human affection, had clung to him and pulled him into the cot with her. Feeling sleepy was no excuse. Yes, she had been floating in that place, somewhere between wake and sleep, but she knew perfectly well what she was doing. It was a terrible risk of course but who knew if she would survive this voyage? It didn't seem like the time to second guess her wants and needs. Whatever became of her, she would never forget how safe she had felt cradled in Nash's strong arms. She was lucky he was gentleman enough not to take advantage of her. Though, after their almost-kiss before the attack broke out, she wondered if she was more likely to take advantage of him than the other way around. For reasons she could not understand she was sensitive to this man's touch, not to mention his piercing stare, in a way she never expected to be.

'Having known me for less than two days, Mr Nash, I don't think you have any idea what I do or do not deserve.'

'Matter of fact, I do. I'm an excellent judge of character.'

'Is that so,' Bronwyn said, bathing his wound and at the same time noticing again the roundness of the captain's tummy. It was covered in soft, dark hair too. She wouldn't have expected to find such a quality attractive and yet there was something about it that made her want to reach out and stroke him. Perhaps that soft down is what had made resting her body against his so comfortable last night.

'Yes, and you deserve more than the treatment you've had from me.'

'Then why not let me go?'

'I can't.'

'Of course you can. You're the captain. One word from you and the crew will turn the boat around and have me back in Pembroke by tea time tomorrow.'

'If you think that, you don't know very much about pirates,' said Nash, shaking his head. 'Price owes me for past misdemeanours and the crew want their cut.'

'You've alluded to that before, when you had a sword to my throat as I recall. What terrible thing did Leonard do to you that I have to pay so steep a price for?'

'We will speak of that later.'

'That's what you said last night,' said Bronwyn. 'If I'm being held captive against my will, I think I at least deserve to know why.'

Miles opened his mouth to speak but then hesitated. 'Are you sure you're ready to know the truth about the man you're going to marry?'

Bronwyn pursed her lips. She had already decided, of course, that she would not marry Price after the way he had cowered when threatened by Nash and his crew, leaving her vulnerable to his attack. But it was likely imprudent to convey this information to Nash. He seemed to have some strange admiration for her but she would be a fool to trust a kidnapper. If he knew she didn't intend to go through with her marriage, he might believe this would somehow disrupt his plan to extort Price, and who knows what would happen to her then?

'If I didn't want to know, I wouldn't have asked.'

A pause followed in which Nash studied her closer than she'd like.

'He killed my love,' Nash said at last, in a tone of voice that made Bronwyn's blood run cold.

She stared at him a moment and swallowed hard before speaking again. 'Are you accusing my betrothed of murder?'

'In a manner of speaking.'

'What does that mean?'

'It means he's not merciful enough to put a dagger through a person's heart. Consorting with him offers a slow, long death. And that's what happened to my Cecily. He stole her fortune. He drove her mad. She died of heartbreak and neglect. Price has to pay for that and, no matter what, I swear he will.'

Not knowing quite what to say, Bronwyn began tearing strips off her now ragged wedding gown and tied the make-shift bandage around the captain's waist as best she could.

'You don't believe me, do you?' Nash said.

Bronwyn considered her response. Nash's description of Price didn't fit the gentle suitor she had known all of these weeks. One who had been respectful of the fact that she could never love another again the way she had loved Alexander. He had suggested a kindly partnership after the death of her mother which, he had calmly explained, would be of much support given her father had already passed on too. Price promised to be someone who would guide and support her and, as thanks for agreeing to marry a scarred bride, Price would take control of the family granite mine which had truly flourished in the last decade and was on the brink of yet more great fortune.

Still, Price had hardly been chivalrous when they were beset by pirates and Nash must be going to all this trouble of kidnapping her for some reason. It was fair to say this whole episode had made her reassess her prior understanding of Leonard Price.

'The truth is a funny thing,' Bronwyn said. 'It is different things to different people. I was not there so cannot speak as to what happened.'

'What you mean is, you'll take the word of a gentleman over the word of a dirty pirate.'

Bronwyn finally met Nash's eyes and was surprised to see the hurt flaring in them. The fact that she had not outright believed him seemed to have cut him deeper than she would have expected. She didn't understand why witnessing the suffering of a man who kidnapped her should bring her anything but satisfaction. But satisfaction was nowhere to be found. Whatever the reality of his situation with Cecily, there was no ignoring the fact that Nash was a man in torment.

She stood and, much as he had with her the night before, she brushed the loose strands of hair gently out of his face. 'Miles, if that is what I meant, that is what I would have said.'

Again, at the use of his first name, he blinked in surprise. The hurt in his eyes seemed to diminish somewhat and Bronwyn was certain she saw a glimmer of light flicker in them. A glimmer that sparked a surprising heat in her considering conditions were less than tropical on board The

Serpent. On realising how close she was yet again to abandoning all sense of propriety, Bronwyn took a step back from the captain. 'With a bit of luck, you'll heal well enough now.'

Understanding this was his cue to leave, Nash tried to stand but after hours of battle, his strength was lacking.

'Here, I think you had better lie down for a while,' Bronwyn said, setting him down in her cot.

'I will not lie down, I have a ship to command.'

'Really?' Bronwyn said, jabbing him gently in the ribs.

'Yow!' Miles cried out. 'What was that for?'

'That was me underlining the point you're barely in a fit state to command your own feet in the right direction, let alone a ship. Now lie down.'

Muttering under his breath, Nash slumped into her cot as she pulled the thin blanket over him.

'At any rate, I could do with a walk on deck after being cooped up with nothing but the noise of explosions and cries of pain for hours on end.'

'You can't walk the decks alone, it's not safe,' Nash warned.

'I will return before sunset. The crew are well aware of the threats you made to Roberts when he overstepped, and word has probably spread about what I did to his hand. I don't think any of them will be stupid enough to try anything in broad daylight, at least for now. Just rest. It may not look like it, but I can fend for myself.'

She smiled and began to walk towards the door, trying not to think about how severe the captain's wound had looked.

'Bronwyn,' Nash said. She turned to him raising an eyebrow. 'When I take you back to Pembroke, don't marry Price.'

Bronwyn sighed but did not offer him any insights about her thoughts on that matter. 'Rest now, Captain,' was all she would say before closing the door behind her.

CHAPTER SIX

The sun was almost setting when Miles made his way out on deck. He scanned the ship for Bronwyn and at last set eyes on her, looking out across the ocean not far from the bow of the boat. The sky was a rich blend of orange and pink and with the wind whipping through her hair and a green silk dress billowing all around her, Bronwyn looked nothing short of entrancing.

Thank the saints Rookwood had finally found a dress for the lady to wear among the loot they had stowed. Of course, she looked even more ravishing than she had when parts of her captivating form were showing through the tears of her tattered wedding gown. But at least now when he looked at her, he no longer had to think of Price. Or of the fact that when the thirty days were up he would have to give this seemingly sensitive soul back to him. He had spent the hours between the battle and now breathing in the scent of ripe grapefruit she had left in her cot. How the bed smelled so strongly of her after she had spent but one night in it, he couldn't say. Perhaps because he willed it so. In any case, his lungs were still full of it, full of her and he realised he was happy for it.

Over the hours that had passed since she tended his wound, he had thought many times about how her name had sounded on his lips. She had uttered it twice, softly, affectionately, and as she did so something inside him had begun to ache. It had also caused him to imagine how she might sound when she was moaning his name, or perhaps even screaming it.

Miles marched up to where she was standing, despite the stinging in his stomach as he did so, and took a hip flask of rum from his pocket. He had laid off the drink while he'd had Bronwyn on board. He had thought it best to stay lucid in case she tried to escape or any other of his crew members tried to defile the woman as Roberts had. But right now he needed the drink to take the edge off the pain.

As he approached, he noticed Dodger lying near the lady. He looked up at his master with vacant eyes as though he had never seen him before. Miles shook his head at the beast. If it weren't for him, Dodger would still be picking at chicken bones on the New York docks. At the same time however, he could not blame the mutt for being captivated with Bronwyn. Though he could never act on his feelings, Miles couldn't deny that he felt the same.

'You were to return to your cabin at sunset, I believe,' he said to her.

She turned in such a way that the westerly wind ruffled her long blonde hair in just the way he longed to. 'The sun has not quite set yet, Captain. But must you undo all the hard work I did treating you by dancing about the deck in the chill.'

Miles grinned and shook his flask at her. 'Rum will keep me warm. Are you cold though, lady? Why, yes you are. I can see your skin pimpling. Here,' Miles took off his jacket and wrapped it around Brownyn's shoulders. It would seem like a chivalrous enough gesture but in truth it wasn't entirely selfless. Seeing Bronwyn's creamy shoulders on display was giving him ideas he knew were pointless to have.

'Thank you,' she said, pulling the coat close around her. 'You know, had you not kidnapped me, I would apologise for suggesting that your kindnesses were an act.'

Miles frowned and took a gulp of rum before responding. 'I am not the most learned man but I deem that a confusing sentence. Are you apologising for misjudging me?'

'Certainly not. I would never apologise to a man who had held a sword to my throat and brought me to the one place in all the world that would torture me.'

'My ship is the one place in all the world that would torture you?'

'Not your ship, the ocean,' Bronwyn said, pointing out at the vast blue.

'Why do you hate the ocean?'

'For the same reason you hate my fiancé.'

Hearing Bronwyn refer to Price as her fiancé after how he had warned her about him made Miles's blood boil, but he managed to keep his tone civil. 'I do not follow.'

'The ocean killed my love,' said Bronwyn.

'Al –'

Bronwyn shot him a look more piercing than any dagger.

'He... drowned?'

Bronwyn nodded. 'He was handsome, you might remember me telling you.'

'Yes,' Miles said, trying not to grit his teeth as he did so. God's blood! How could he be jealous of a dead man?

'But he wasn't rich, at least not in the long run. He was supposed to inherit from his father but... his father didn't approve of me. Thought there was a better match out there for his son and cut him out of his inheritance.'

Miles sighed and shook his head. 'I'm sorry. Clearly your beloved had a great deal more sense than his father.'

'I begged Alex not to choose me over his future, or at least be content that my father's granite mine would keep a roof over our head, but of course he wouldn't hear of it. Instead, he joined the Navy. Planned to be away for three years in the first instance and earn enough that he might feel like he could truly provide for me and any babes we might have. But his ship was lost. There were no survivors.'

Miles studied Bronwyn's face. She was close to tears. More than anything he wanted to take her in his arms and comfort her. She had been through so much and, thanks to him, she would go through a lot more before the month was out.

'I don't know what to say,' was all he managed.

'Say you will take me back to shore.'

'What?'

'I did not tell you about my most private loss for sympathy, Captain. I spoke of Alexander so you would be under no illusions about the emotional duress you will put me under if you do not return me to St Davids. That every day you make me a pawn in your game with Price, you cause me unspeakable suffering. Don't you see? If it were not for me, Alex would yet live. With every sway of this boat and every glimpse of the ocean I am reminded of what I lost, and that I was to blame.'

Miles frowned and took hold of her arms. 'Hear me now: what happened to your love was not your fault. He sailed towards fortune because he wanted to provide for you, something any man would wish to do. I know the ocean and she is a force you can neither predict nor control. What happened to Alex was not your failing.'

'Will you take me home or not?' Bronwyn said, her blue eyes full of tears.

'I cannot do that, even though I am not unmoved by your tale. I have come too far now, the crew would kill us both if I tried to turn this boat around.'

Bronwyn's eyes narrowed. 'I don't believe you, you just want your revenge and you'll clearly put me through anything to get it.'

'And why shouldn't I have my revenge for what your betrothed did to the woman I loved? You dare to call me a liar again when you know my heart has been broken just as surely as yours has?'

'Your heart? Broken?' Bronwyn snapped, tearing off Miles's coat and shoving it hard enough into his chest to shunt him backwards. 'You have to have one first, Captain.' She bustled past him towards her cabin and Dodger loped after her.

'Bronwyn!' Miles called, as he gave chase, but she continued into her cabin and, once over the threshold, curled up in her cot.

'Just lock the door,' she said. 'I am your captive after all.'

Sighing, Miles did as she instructed. No sooner had he turned the key in the lock than he heard her gentle sobs. A sound so desperate that, though Miles would not have thought it possible, fractured his broken heart into smaller pieces than it had been before.

CHAPTER SEVEN

The next afternoon Bronwyn stood on the starboard side of the ship, filling her lungs with fresh air as best she could. Nash had barely grunted when he opened her door that morning. After their bitter exchange the day before, the brute was at last showing the indifference to her suffering she had known he felt all along. It was a relief, in a way. Somehow it pained her to think of him as possessing a noble heart. But she knew now he had no such qualities. If he did, he would have taken her back to port when he had learned what she had suffered with Alex. Now that he had dropped the act she could focus on doing what she had intended from the start: avoiding him as much as possible.

The sun beat down hard on her bare shoulders as she looked out to the horizon. Blue in every direction. Not a scrap of land. No other ship.

Just the tormenting ocean on all sides. Sighing, she stared down into the choppy depths that had claimed the man she loved, and scorned herself again for not being more forceful about him finding work in St Davids. If she had persuaded Alex to stay she would be far from the clutches of Nash and his crew, and Alex would still be alive. At that thought she could have sworn she saw a shadow flit beneath the waves. She leaned over the sill of the ship a little further, studying the waves more closely. She supposed it was a fish of some nature. Or maybe a dolphin. But then, several feet from where the ship's hull cut through sea, a figure surfaced. Just a head and a pair of shoulders. Water dripped slowly from the figure's ear-length dark hair. From his angular cheek bones. He looked up at Bronwyn and held a finger to his perfect lips. Warning her to keep her peace.

'Alex...' she whispered to herself. She looked harder at the man in the water. Could it really be him? Of course it was. She would never mistake those green-grey eyes for those of another. He had come back from the dead itself, to rescue her.

A smile spread across his face as he seemed to guess her realisation. How foolish she had been to lose faith that he would find a way to reach her, even beyond death.

With a single finger he beckoned her into the water to join him.

Bronwyn's smile slackened. Silly girl. Alex hadn't come back from the dead, that would have been too much of a happy ever after. Such miracles never happened. He had instead, she theorised, come to claim her and take her with him to the underworld. He had beckoned her because he wanted her to sacrifice herself to the merciless ocean, just as he had. So they could be together on the other side of all this. Far away from Nash and Price and whatever feud raged between them. All she had to do was swing her legs over the edge of the boat and let go.

Without checking to see if anyone might see her, Bronwyn eased herself up onto the ledge and swung her legs over so they dangled above the surf. Sea foam swirled below and she was suddenly aware of how fast the boat was moving. Much swifter than she had ever guessed while she stood on the other side of the railing. She couldn't say how far the drop was either.

Twenty feet perhaps, if she were forced to guess. She looked back out to the ocean again where Alex had surfaced. He was still there but was beginning to submerge.

Perhaps he could only spend so long in this world before he was taken back to the other side? She had to act quickly if she was going to catch his hand and follow him to the beyond.

Closing her eyes, Bronwyn pushed herself off the side of the boat and fell, so much harder and so much further than she had thought she would. The green satin of the dress Rookwood had found for her, rippled around her ears. Her stomach seemed to push against her throat, and all breath had been ripped from her lungs so that she could not have screamed even if she wanted to.

At last she hit the water and just managed to catch a deep breath before the ocean shot icy darts into every inch of her skin. Not that she need have bothered taking such a breath. How much breath she had in her lungs would not matter for long. Soon the water would claim her and so would Alex. She opened her eyes and squinting through the darkness she saw a shimmering vision of Alex, his dark hair, which seemed to be longer under water, floating around him as he reached out to her. She swam a few strokes in his direction, and reached out. Her feet kept entangling themselves in her petticoat so it took much effort to move even just a short distance. Every time she thought she was close enough to touch his hand the current seemed to pull him further away. At last she fancied she had gained enough purchase to touch him again. She stretched out her delicate fingers. They were less than an inch from his when the world around Bronwyn turned black.

CHAPTER EIGHT

oman overboard! Starboard side!'

The sound of those words called down by Jimmy, sickened Miles to his stomach. Throwing down the fishing nets he had been about to cast, he dashed to starboard, alongside several of the crew members. Down below in the water he could see the dark shadow of Bronwyn's body just beneath the surface of the waves.

'God's blood!' Miles bellowed, shirking off his long coat. 'Lower the jolly boat, now!'

The men made short work of lowering the small skiff that hung on davits not far from the stern. But it was clear it was going to take too long to lower it completely. Without a second thought to his own safety, Miles took a deep breath and dove into the Atlantic, trying to ignore thoughts of what might happen if he didn't get to Bronwyn in time.

It was murky, deep beneath the surface. He twisted and thrashed, searching for some small glimpse of her. Her delicate fingers. A billow of green fabric. An ankle he could latch onto. For a few moments Miles couldn't see much of anything. But then his eyes adjusted and he caught a flash of Bronwyn's body silhouetted by what little sunlight filtered through the dimness at this depth. Her blonde hair spread out on the water above him. Ignoring the strain on his lungs, he swam towards her and reached out a hand. He managed to grab hold of an arm. His eyes widened, despite the immediate sting of salt water. It felt limp.

Terror coursed through Miles's veins. He had to get her to the surface now.

Wrapping an arm around her waist, he swam with one arm, dragging her upwards as fast as his thrashing legs could propel him. A soft glimmer of light grew brighter just before they broke through the waves and the sun glared at them.

At the sight of their captain successfully retrieving their cargo, a cheer rang out from the crew still on deck. Miles however, feared it was far too soon for celebration. Bronwyn still lay flaccid in his arm, her head lolling, still not speaking, still not breathing.

He scanned the water for the jolly boat and on spotting it tugged her over. With little grace he managed push her over the side and using the last of his might he pulled himself up onto the boat too. He lay panting for just a few moments, clutching at his wound which had only now begun to pain him, before crawling over to where Bronwyn lay, lifeless and pale.

'Bronwyn,' he said, moving her tangled hair from her face and shaking her shoulders.

Her skin felt like ice.

Her face blank of all expression.

'Pat her back, Cap'n,' Rookwood yelled down. 'I've seen it work once or twice with a body full of water.

Miles moved behind her and, as instructed, manoeuvred Bronwyn into a slumped sitting position. Her head fell forward. He patted her wet bodice. Softly at first and then more vigorously, as hard as he dare hit a lady. When she didn't respond, Miles wrapped his arms around her waist and squeezed her close to him. Her body still felt icy against his chest, even beneath the warmth of the afternoon sun.

'Bronwyn, please,' he murmured urgently in her ears. 'Please come back to me.'

Powerless to do more, he rocked her gently from side to side. To Miles's surprise, tears threatened behind his lids as she remained silent and still.

This was utterly his fault. Unable to control his feelings around her, he had tried to distance himself and now without his careful watch she had come to harm. He tried not to think of how she had so fearlessly run back into a burning building to save her sister when she was young, changing her life forever. Or how she had undeservingly lost the man she loved. Or how she had practically begged him to return her to shore after explaining that life at sea was perpetual torment for her.

Gently, he tried to smooth the tangles of her wet hair. This lady's last days were spent enduring a cruelty he could have found a way to prevent, if he hadn't been so cowardly about standing up to his crew. When she came to him, he should have declared the kidnap over with a promise they would find some other way to extort Price.

He was just about to prepare himself for the fact that Bronwyn was not going to awaken when her body jolted with a choking sound. She coughed up what looked like an entire ocean. He watched with joy as she spluttered and gasped for air before starting to violently shiver.

'She's alive!' Miles yelled up to the crew. Hoist us up, quick quick! At once.'

As the crew did as they were commanded, Bronwyn, who was still understandably bewildered and blinking, began to sob. Unable to bear the sound, Miles wrapped his arms tighter around her and even took the liberty of kissing the side of her wet head, making sure he was not in view of the crew as he did so. The relief surging through him at her revival was like nothing he had felt before and he relished the excuse to hold Bronwyn's delicate form against his chest. Shivering, she curled up into him and clutched at his shirt then buried her head in his neck. The pressure of her body made his wound smart all the more but he didn't care. He was in much more torture over the nearness of her lips. What he would give to kiss them. To worship her body. To let her know he was sorry. For the kidnapping. For his obsession with revenge. For his unwillingness to end her suffering. But alas, he could indulge not one of these impulses. He may have just saved her life but if it weren't for him her life wouldn't have needed to be saved

The moment they were in reach, Miles lifted Bronwyn up to Rookwood and the reaching hands of the crew who safely received the lady. They then reached back to pull Miles over the ledge. The second he was on deck he threw his coat around Bronwyn and, unlike yesterday, she showed no signs of throwing it back at him.

'I will take her to my quarters where she can warm by the fire,' Miles told the rest of the crew. 'In my absence, I trust you'll do all you can to catch some fish for supper.'

'Captain,' Rookwood said, beckoning Miles in a manner that implied what he had to say was for his ears only.

With some reluctance, Miles sat Bronwyn down on a nearby barrel and strode over to Rookwood. 'Yes?'

'I think the lady's days of sunning herself on the deck might be at an end, if we want our treasure that is. According to Jimmy, she did not fall into the sea. She jumped.'

'Jumped?' Miles said, glancing back at Bronwyn. Had the torture she felt over Alex's death really become so unbearable? And was death really preferable to life with him on this ship? That thought stung Miles more than he could bear. Or perhaps she had jumped out of spite after he wouldn't take her back to shore? She may have decided that if she wasn't going to get her way, he wouldn't get what he wanted either. Miles was not one for swift judgments. But whatever the reason Bronwyn leapt to her death, he intended to find out what it was.

CHAPTER NINE

ash had given Bronwyn the privacy to change in her own quarters while he lit the fire in his. He had also left a dry banyan of black silk on her cot, thoughtful but necessary given she had nothing else to wear. She assumed it was his. Certainly, it carried his scent. Sitting by the fire and feeling her saturated hair slowly dry, Bronwyn tried to make sense of what had happened when she jumped into the Atlantic. Had she died for a moment there? She couldn't be sure. If she had, there hadn't been any light waiting for her. She remembered the world fading to black and then nothing. Nothing at all. The next time she felt light and warmth was when she realised she was in Nash's arms.

'Here,' Nash said, handing her a hot cup of what looked like coffee.

Bronwyn took a tentative sip then pulled a face. 'What's in this?'

'It's just coffee,' said Nash, amusement glowing in his amber eyes. 'With a jot of rum of course.'

'Oh, of course,' Bronwyn said, her tone dryly mocking. 'Heaven forbid you ever drink anything free of rum.' She had hoped that they would manage to keep things light. The last thing she wanted to do was talk about what she had done. But a few moments after her comment she saw the glow in Nash's eyes dim.

'Was the prospect of twenty-eight more days in my company so terrible to you that a watery grave seemed more appealing?'

'I do not wish to talk about it.'

'You have no hope of avoiding the topic. I need to know, must I keep you locked away? Will you try to throw yourself overboard at every opportunity?'

'No! I only jumped because...'

'Because what?' Nash said, pushing a hand through his sandy waves. As he did so, Bronwyn caught herself wondering what it would feel like to run her fingers through that hair and had to actively work to clear her mind of such thoughts.

'God's blood Bronwyn,' Nash continued. 'I am responsible for your wellbeing on this ship.

You will tell me everything I need to know to keep you safe.'

'You know all you need to know, it won't happen again.'

Nash sighed, seemingly understanding she was not going to have a cosy chat with the man who put her in this predicament in the first place. In what looked like defeat, he sat down by the fire just a foot or so away from where Bronwyn was curled up. She took a deep breath and stared into the flames. There was something calming about the fierce orange flickering, and anything was better than looking at Nash by the fire's glow. She knew his sandy hair would turn to gold in such lighting and his amber eyes would themselves become burning flames she could not resist.

'I think it's time you told me why you're putting me through the suffering of this voyage,' Bronwyn said.

'I already have,' said Nash.

'Only in the vaguest of terms,' said Bronwyn, at last daring to look at him. Just as she had thought, the firelight only made him more alluring. More kissable. 'You say my fiancé killed your love. I want to know what you mean by that. Are you saying he murdered her?'

'That would have been humane,' Nash almost growled. 'And that is not in Price's nature.'

'Miles, what did he do? You may as well tell me if you wish for me to be in anyway cooperative for the remainder of the trip.'

Nash sighed at the use of his first name. Whenever she spoke it, it seemed to work like some magic chant, leaving him no choice but to tell her whatever she wanted.

'Cecily was a bright, beautiful, educated woman,' said Nash. 'I met her in New York some seven years back now. Given her considerable qualities, not to mention the size of her dowry, she was not short of potential suitors but I fell in love with her the moment we first met at a dance in town. And from that moment, I decided, I'd do everything in my power to win and wed her. Our family were not as well to do as some. My father traded furs. I decided to get into the shipping business which seemed a sure enough bet given how it was booming. For almost two years, I courted Cecily in the gentlemanly fashion expected of me. I spoke at length to her father about my successes in shipping and the kind of house I'd buy to keep Cecily in as much luxury as she deserved. With so many potential suitors available, Cecily's father kept his options open for some time, but all that changed when Price entered our lives.'

'What happened?' Bronwyn asked, though she admitted privately she was afraid to hear the answer.

'Price arrived in New York to a lot of buzz. A titled English Lord in town always set the hearts of the city's mothers aflutter. Given his considerable status, he met with a number of wealthy families, one of which was Cecily's.'

'And I take it Cecily's father thought him a better match for his daughter than any other?'

'He did, but Price left nothing to chance. He wooed Cecily, which was a bitter blow as it was. I had been trying for her hand for almost two years but within a month Cecily begged her father to let her marry Price. Still, when you love someone as I loved Cecily, when it comes down to it you just want their happiness. So, miserable as I was, I accepted that she did not want to spend her life with me.'

Bronwyn noticed Nash's voice falter at those last words. Despite his claims of good sportsmanship, the wound he'd sustained from a rejection by the woman he loved, was clearly still raw.

'From what I understood,' Nash continued once he'd recomposed himself. 'Price had showered her in soft words and mighty promises, and she had no reason to not take him at his word. Neither did myself or any of her friends. Several months after they were married however, I encountered Cecily buying bread at one of the markets. Only she didn't have the money she needed to pay for it. I paid for the bread and walked with her by the docks. I almost didn't recognise the woman. She was so much thinner than she had been. Her face was drawn. She had black circles around her eyes and her hair was unattended to.'

Bronwyn frowned. 'Why couldn't she afford bread when she had a sizeable dowry, and Leonard has money enough to keep them both for the rest of their lives? He doesn't even need to marry someone with a large dowry.'

'She told me he had frittered away her money in a matter of weeks and refused to delve into his own fortune. His prior gentlemanly nature had dissolved the minute they were married.'

'Couldn't she go to her parents?'

'She said she had tried. But they told her she was a wife now and that she was beholden to her husband. She had to trust he was doing the best for her.'

'I don't understand, why wouldn't they help their daughter?'

'They had made it clear that the shame of divorce or separation would be a smirch on the family name. She had begged them to marry Price, and he was a rich man so they didn't understand her quarrels.'

'How frightening for her,' said Bronwyn. Three days ago she wouldn't have believed the pirate's story about her betrothed. Leonard Price had been the model of a perfect gentleman. But Bronwyn couldn't help but remember how Price had reacted when Nash had descended on their wedding. His first thought had been for himself. That had told her all she needed to know. Nash may have kidnapped her but he had shown true warmth and kindness in that time and though her kidnap was not forgivable, if he had done it to avenge the death of a woman he loved it was at least an understandable action. If someone had killed Alex there was no doubt she would have pursued the culprit and not stopped until justice was served. At that thought Bronwyn realised that she still hadn't heard the full story. 'How did Cecily die? 'Did you try to help her?'

Nash nodded. 'I told her I would sail her away on one of the ships we used for trading.'

Bronwyn's eyes widened. 'It was this ship, wasn't it? That you were going to sail her away on.'

Again Nash offered a nod. The captain's choice of ship made more sense to her now. It was large enough, but not as large as some of the pirate ships Bronwyn had heard about. And there weren't as many canons on board as she would have expected. She had counted thirty-six on each side – seventy-two in total. Perhaps this wasn't so small a number but she had heard of many ships having closer to one hundred and fifty guns.

'Did… did something happen to Cecily at sea, as it did with Alex?'

'We didn't get that far,' Nash said. 'We had planned to sail the very next day. She was going to collect what few belongings she had left and meet me at the docks the next morning. When she didn't arrive, I knew something was wrong.

I had word later that day that Cecily had been found dead in her chamber. She had taken cyanide.'

'That's... well, there aren't words for how terrible that is. But why did she resort to that when she had an escape with you?'

'She had a short note sent to me before she ended her life. She had been too afraid to tell me that she was pregnant with Price's child. She said she knew when I found out, I couldn't love a child belonging to Price and she did not want to have his child in any case. When I read that letter, I thought I would burst with anger. I marched to Cecily's house and beat at the door until a servant, who probably knew everything that had unfolded, answered and allowed me to see Price.'

'He lived to leave New York, that much I know, so you must have managed to control your rage... at least enough to leave him alive,' said Bronwyn.

'The only thing that kept me in check was knowing that if I lost control and tried to injure or kill him Price would have succeeded in ruining my life as well as Cecily's. Of course, I didn't know then that I would be reduced to piracy. If I had known, I should have killed him and gladly hung for it.'

'Don't say that. Please,' said Bronwyn, unable to stop herself from imagining his body hanging in the market square, surrounded by cackling townsfolk throwing their rotten fruit.

'I introduced myself properly to Price and told him to remember my name. I told him I knew what he had done to Cecily and that one day, thanks to me, he would live to regret it.'

'How did Price respond?'

'He laughed. The bastard laughed as though I was his entertainment. It took me four years to get all the information and resources I needed but I kept my word and no matter what choice he makes when I go back to St Davids, he won't be smiling when I'm through.'

Bronwyn raised her eyebrows, remembering the choice Nash had given Price before he had hustled her out of the cathedral. 'Neither will I if you cut my throat and let me bleed to death on the sands.'

'That won't happen,' Miles said, an urgent note in his voice. 'It was a threat designed to put pressure on Price to hand over his riches. That's the only thing he cares about in this world so that's what I'm taking from him. No harm will come to you, or the villages of Pembroke, you have my word.'

Bronwyn took a deep breath and wondered how much the word of a pirate was worth. When she looked at him again he was staring into the flames, almost in a trance-like state. 'Cecily was wrong. I would have loved that child as if it was my own, just as I loved her. Neither of them had to die.'

A single tear slid down Nash's cheek and in that moment, he didn't look at all like a fearsome pirate. He was just another broken-hearted soul, like Bronwyn. Slowly, she crawled over to where he was sitting. It wasn't a rational action, it was pure instinct that led her to put her arms around his neck. 'I'm so very sorry you lost her,' she said.

CHAPTER TEN

iles circled his arms around Bronwyn's waist, pulled her closer into his lap and thanked God she didn't resist him. He had not known such relief in as long as he could remember. Not just because holding her fragile little body made him feel strong but because she had sympathised with him over the loss of Cecily. Which meant, at the very least, she understood why he had been so callous as to kidnap her.

'I thought you were gone, dead in the water,' Miles said, looking into her stormy blue eyes. 'I thought my thirst for revenge had killed you. I felt so empty.'

'If I had died, it would not have been your fault,' said Bronwyn. 'At least, not directly. I jumped because I thought... I thought I saw Alex. I thought he had come to find me and take me to the afterlife. My, it sounds so idiotic to say it out loud. But you must understand losing

Alex has haunted me for so long, even more so since I stepped foot on this ship.'

Nash shook his head. 'You need not explain. I have seen Cecily splashing amongst the waves many times, the sea can do strange things to our senses.'

Bronwyn nodded. 'Certainly I am not myself on this ship. Befriending a pirate, holding him close no less. You'll no doubt think me a wanton.'

She went to remove herself from his lap but Miles held her in place. 'I would think no such thing,' he paused. 'Do you want me to let you go?'

At his question her whole body stiffened. He could not tell precisely what caused this reaction but from the manner in which her eyes had widened, Miles could only guess that she was in some kind of war with herself over what her answer should be.

'Because I would much rather hold you close than let you go,' he prompted.

'Why?' she said, her eyes narrowing abruptly.

He wanted to laugh at her suspicious demeanour but sensed now was not the time. 'I do not have an easy answer to that,' he said.

'All I know is that I feel at peace when we are holding each other. That I find you captivating, and I have not found any woman captivating... since Cecily.'

'Nobody?' Bronwyn said, the arching of her eyebrows betraying the deepening of her suspicions. 'Isn't that rare for a pirate? Aren't women supposed to slip through your fingers as easy as the gold you plunder?'

'You forget, I am not a real pirate. This ship, this crew, this guise, they are all only to serve the purpose of revenge. We have taken other ships as a means of survival while I have gathered information on Price's riches and whereabouts. But in the last four years I have been singular in my purpose without any time for distractions.'

'Oh...' Bronwyn said. A peculiar expression, impossible to read, crossed over her face.

'Am I to take it by that look that you have yet more questions for me?'

Bronwyn half-smiled at this. 'It's just that you and Cecily never...' She pushed her hands together as she spoke in what seemed to be a symbolic gesture. 'Does that mean you've never...?'

Oh this woman was too outrageous for words. Was she actually asking him if he had ever spent the night strumming?

'I didn't feel it fitting for a pirate captain to have no understanding of such matters so I took the liberty of visiting a whore before we set sail from New York, some years ago. It was an experience I'd sooner forget. It was not how I imagined it. Is that a full enough answer for you, Princess?' Miles said, leaning forward so that his lips hovered over hers.

'Good enough,' she said. The hitch in her breath told him she found being close to him as intoxicating as he found being close to her.

'Any more questions?'

'Just one.'

'I'm listening.'

'Will you kiss me, Miles?'

Though the question was bold, the poor woman looked petrified. As though she feared he might refuse her. Clearly his open fascination had been lost on her.

He moved his mouth even closer so that his lips brushed against hers as he spoke. 'Nothing would give me greater pleasure, Princess.'

Unable to hold himself back for even another moment, Miles closed the distance between them and pressed his lips against Bronwyn's. The sensation that rushed through him in that moment almost took his breath away completely. It was true, what he had told her, about his experience with women being somewhat limited but every moment she had been aboard his ship he had thought of yet another way he would like to kiss her, touch her, take her. Consequently, when Bronwyn so readily opened her mouth to him and teased his lips with her tongue, he met her tongue with his and groaned hard as her kiss became harder, almost savage in its intensity.

He pushed back against her with equal force and in another moment, his hands were in her hair, stroking the soft golden waves, still damp and smelling of the ocean that had beckoned to him so often. Bronwyn returned the gesture. Tangling her fingers in his hair, and tugging just hard enough to betray her need for him.

He moved his lips from hers then and concentrated on kissing the scars along her face before moving down to her neck. As he kissed and lightly nibbled her skin her hands moved to his back and he felt her nails digging into his flesh. Something about the sharp sting made his rod strain against his breeches. Without another thought he lay Bronwyn on her back in front of the fire. It was only then he remembered that she was dressed in nothing more than his banyon. All he need do was undo the buttons and her whole body would be laid bare for him to kiss and suck and lick to his heart's content.

'I want to kiss you, Bronwyn,' he whispered.

Bronwyn scrunched up her face. 'You are kissing me.'

'Not just here,' he said, pressing two fingers to her lips before trailing them down her chin, along her neck to the collar of his banyon. 'Every single inch of you.'

Again, her breathing faltered in a manner that hinted pure desire. He needed no other invitation to undo the top button. 'Tell me to stop.'

Bronwyn shook her head. 'I don't want you to stop.'

Slowly Miles continued to open each button one by one, with every passing moment revealing another stretch of perfectly pale flesh. When at last there were no more buttons to open, he pulled the fabric aside and could barely believe what he saw. Two pert breasts, a dreamy curve at the waist and hips that could bear children with little effort. The animal in him wanted to part her thighs there and then for a closer look at what hid there, but it was too soon to unleash that side of himself. He needed to gain her trust. For now, she would have the gentleman and then, if that went well, he would see about introducing her to the other things he had imagined.

'You are beyond beautiful,' he said as his eyes roamed her body. Bronwyn looked at him. He could tell from the way her breasts rocked gently back and forth, that she was breathing deep and fast. The shocking pink of her nipples against her otherwise moon-pale flesh mesmerised him. He hoped her erratic breathing was a result of exhilaration rather than fear but to be sure, he moved to lean over her and kissed her soft, sensuous lips. 'Remember, I am new to this,' he murmured. 'So tell me, when I am pleasing you and don't hesitate to direct me on how to pleasure you more thoroughly.'

Bronwyn looked quite astonished by his words. So astonished in fact that he wondered if it were not seemly to ask a woman to openly describe what would most please them. Given his somewhat limited experience, that was the only way he could imagine learning and what a pleasurable apprenticeship it would be. He flashed her a smile just before his lips travelled south again and watched a look of aching ecstasy replaced the surprise on her face. Grabbing one of her breasts in his firm hand and clamping his mouth around the nipple of the other, he breathed in her warmth and fruity fragrance. Her body arched and her hips jolted into him in such a way that it was clear their time together was off to an encouraging start.

CHAPTER ELEVEN

'Oh, God, Miles!' Bronwyn moaned as she watched his tongue circling her nipples. He then covered them with his mouth and sucked hungrily. Was this really happening? How had this happened so quickly? Though he was the one who had undressed her, she had started it all when she had so brazenly asked him to kiss her. A bold move that she would not ordinarily have made but she had died today, or very nearly, and she hadn't seen the bright, heavenly light she was expecting. If there was nothing more than this, she wasn't going to waste a minute of it. She had no idea quite how far Miles planned to take this but in that moment she found herself blithely unconcerned about that matter. She had only joined with Alex once before he had left for sea but she remembered how alive it had made her feel. She wanted to feel that way again, with Miles.

His amber eyes sparkled up at her as he kissed his way down her tummy. His expression was so odd, and alluring. He seemed both content and starving all at once. She reached a hand down to tangle her fingers in his hair, which was softer to the touch than she ever could have imagined. And oh, the length of it was just as enticing. Long enough to tug. She writhed as his beard tickled her navel, leaving her wondering how it would feel against her inner thigh when he began kissing her in the places she truly desired. She lifted her hips to meet his mouth as he licked his way down, down, down.

'You taste of the ocean,' he groaned. 'Only warmer and sweeter.'

But that was the last word she heard from him before he placed his hands under her buttocks and lifted her an inch or two off the floorboards to grant his tongue better access. The sensation of his beard and his tongue dancing so ceaselessly over her most intimate nooks was enough to almost push her over the edge as it was. But then she felt his hands slide from her rear, along her thighs, spreading her legs wider so he might push his tongue deeper. Bronwyn moaned and whimpered and thrashed in response, thrusting her hips helplessly, desperately into Miles's face and all the while those amber eyes watched her naked form twist and jerk at his every caress.

Just when she thought she could not reach a higher plain of pleasure, Miles began to tease her rear entrance with his fingers. Her eyes widened as she wondered what he might do next and a moment later he pushed what felt like his thumb, wet from her arousal, inside. It took Bronwyn a moment to recover from the shock of such a bold gesture on his part. Of all the things she thought he might do with her, she had not expected that.

But then he surprised her yet again.

'If I had another hand spare, I would grab those beautiful breasts. But alas, my fingers are otherwise engaged. So I want you to squeeze your own breasts. Do you hear me?'

'Yes...' The word shuddered out of Bronwyn as she did as he instructed and gripped her breasts, pinching just hard enough to draw pleasure.

'Good girl,' Miles said, before teasing his thumb in and out of her rear and lapping at her slit with increased speed.

It wasn't long before Bronwyn felt her body begin to quake. Her moans turned to ragged screams and she felt herself riding towards a peak more intense than any she could remember.

'Please don't stop, please don't stop!' she begged him breathlessly as she grabbed hold of his hair, pushed his face hard against her and slipped over the edge of a most violent climax.

CHAPTER TWELVE

iles gently kissed his way back up Bronwyn's shivering body, first just below the knee, then at the hip, then between her breasts and at last on her lips which had but moments before emitted some of the most primal sounds he had ever heard. He could barely believe what he had experienced. He would long remember the moment when she did as she was told and squeezed those deliciously pert breasts. The taste of her, the scent, the sound of her lustrous moans, it all drove him wild beyond anything he could have imagined. Oh, how he had wanted to pull down his breeches and take her as she lay there, quivering because of the power he had commanded over her body. But he'd had to restrain himself. If he had taken her it would have risked a child. And given that Miles wasn't entirely sure where he stood with the lady, it seemed imprudent to put her honour in such jeopardy. This logic did not make him ache for her any less however and he wondered how he would control himself if he was to remain in her company for much longer.

Rolling onto his side he drew her into him and kissed her again. Softly swirling his tongue around hers so she might know how good she had tasted. He couldn't quite understand why but kissing her felt so very right. Just as he had imagined it would. Miles had not locked lips with many women but he theorised that it was unlikely to feel this way with everyone.

'That was… that was…'

'I do hope the end of this sentence is good,'

Bronwyn chuckled. 'It's difficult to find a word but I'll settle for unbelievable. If that's what you are capable of when you're new to it, all the women of the world had better watch their step when you've gained more practice.'

'I may not have much direct experience but I have thought about doing that to you since I set eyes on you.'

'What strange tastes in women you have,' Bronwyn teased.

'And you, strange tastes in men.' He laughed and nuzzled into her nose. Doing so almost took his mind off the excruciating throb running all the way down his pole. Almost.

'Ah, but I haven't tasted you… yet.' Bronwyn began lifting Miles's shirt over his head. As she did so he let out an involuntary moan. Was this really happening? Was she going to pleasure him in return as he had pleasured her?

'Oh, did I hurt you?' she asked with a look of genuine fear in her eyes as she surveyed the bandage she had applied to his stomach just the day before.

'No. I'm just… aching for you.'

Her sumptuous lips hitched in a smile as she trailed her tongue down his chest and nibbled playfully on his left nipple. The sensation of her teeth grazing such a sensitive area made the hairs on the back of his neck stand on end.

'Oh Bronwyn,' he growled, 'you minx. The things I could do with a spirited woman such as you.'

Offering no more than a smile, Bronwyn kissed her way down his body, taking pains to avoid his wound, before tearing off his breeches with more expertise than he would have imagined her capable of. Miles knew he had a more substantial belly than most but even over that ample dome he could see the head of his prick standing to attention. Bronwyn stared at it with hunger in her eyes and waited for no invitation before wrapping her wet, warm mouth around him. His whole body arched upward in response, pushing his rod deeper inside her, eager to fill her as far and as deep as he could. Bronwyn swished her tongue around his shaft in response only causing him to swell further as he felt the tip lodge itself in the back of her throat. The contractions as she gagged sent ripples of pleasure right through him but he established eye contact just to be sure he wasn't being too forceful. On meeting his eye she only slid her lips further down the length of him and at once began toying with the sacks between his thighs.

Unable to hold himself back as he watched his rod slide deep into her mouth, his thrusts at once became faster and harder. He knew at this pace the pleasure would all be over too soon and yet he could not force his loins to slow. He wanted, no, needed to pound that feisty little mouth until there was nothing left of him. She swept her hair back giving him an even better view and, realising he could be of some help with this matter, he reached down, grabbed her hair and twisted it around his fist so the sight of his rod filling her mouth so completely was now uninterrupted.

These weren't the mechanical motions of the professional he had visited. Bronwyn was gorging on him. Moaning over the length of him as though she had never tasted anything so luscious. The thought of her taking as much pleasure in him as he had in her pushed him closer to that glorious apex he knew awaited him. Ecstasy was near when she slid her thumb into his rear, just as he had done to her. Miles gasped at the sheer amount of stimulation he was experiencing by her devilish mouth and deft hands.

As though possessed by some greater, animal force utterly beyond his control, he grabbed Bronwyn's head and held her firmly in place. He ground his hips into her face and didn't slow his pace even for a moment until at last he moaned loud enough for every soul on The Serpent to hear. His pole tensed and his every muscle clenched as his hot seed slid down her throat.

His body slackened. Bronwyn circled her tongue around the tip of his rod one last time. He could barely stand the delicious torture of it but he didn't stop her. He liked the idea that even after she had sated him she was hungry for more. With what little strength he had left, Miles pulled Bronwyn into his arms and cradled her body, so pink and warm and soft.

'You will sleep in my bed tonight, Princess,' he murmured into her ear. He expected some argument but instead she just moaned contentedly, in a way that made him want to hold on to her as long as he could, before resting her head in the crook of his neck.

CHAPTER THIRTEEN

The crew had been making jokes about the captain oversleeping for a good hour by the time Bronwyn saw Miles leave the cabin, joining her out on the deck. He looked younger somehow, his face less severe than it had seemed in the preceeding days. Was the light in his eyes burning brighter or was that just her imagination? Her heart clenched at the thought of having to stub out that twinkle. When she had awoken this morning she had at once felt foolish for her actions the night before. Her brush with death had rattled her into feeling that this world was all there was. But she hadn't really died yesterday. She had just come close and as such it was likely a commendable idea to stay on the good side of God. Fill her days with more noble pursuits than providing pirates with oral gratification.

Miles scanned the ship until he noticed her and then marched over at once. Wait, was there a bounce in his step? He *must* be in good sorts after their union last night but it was unfair to lead him on, especially after all he had been through. She had no intention of marrying Price but she wasn't about to marry a pirate either. Besides ensuring the pearly gates would remain open to her, there were also more earthly considerations. She had already lost one man to the ocean, she would not put herself through that again. No matter how perfect his hands had felt on her breasts.

'Good morning,' Miles said, and then added under his breath so that the other crew members couldn't hear, 'Princess.'

A smile spread across Miles's lips that Bronwyn couldn't help return in spite of herself.

'Would you accompany me on a walk to the stern, there are some matters I should like to discuss with you.'

Bronwyn nodded though there was no shaking the sinking feeling as she did so. She had wondered if Miles might have understood her position and maintained an aloof composure, sparing her having to explain to him that last night was in the past and there could be nothing more between them. He was, it seemed, oblivious to the idea that she might be having second thoughts about their tryst but then, after she had moaned and whimpered at his touch so wantonly, she couldn't very well blame him for that.

Following Miles to the stern of the boat, she went over the little speech she had been practicing all morning. As soon as they were out of sight of the crew however, Nash took her completely off-guard with a kiss and pushed her hard against the nearest mast. Bronwyn meant to stop him, truly she did, but the second their lips met she was reminded of how well his mouth fit to hers which in turn only made her think about how well their bodies might do the same.

'Ever since last night,' Miles started to speak between each frantic kiss he planted on her neck, on her cheeks and on her lips, 'I have thought of nothing more than bringing you here to the stern of the boat, lifting you onto my rod and taking you as deep and hard as I like.'

Bronwyn gasped, not only at Miles's outrageous confession but at how arousing she found it. There was no denying the moisture pooling between her thighs at the thought of allowing him to do that to her. 'But what if one of the crew saw us?'

Miles grinned. 'What if they did? I'm big enough to shield you from their prying eyes. But they'd know what I was doing with you of course. They'd no doubt wish themselves into my shoes, not that they would have a chance while I defended your honour.'

A little giggle escaped Bronwyn's lips. A giggle? She didn't giggle. At least, not since Alex had died. There was something about the way Miles had cantered off into his own little fantasy that left her no choice but to laugh. She had the sense from his actions last night that, despite his lack of physical experience, he had some clear ideas about what he wanted to do with a woman when he at last got hold of the right one. But, it seemed, Miles's cravings ran deeper and darker than she had given him credit for.

He wasted not another moment in taking hold of her hands. 'Bronwyn, I have slept so long this morning because I was awake for much of the night thinking through our predicament and I believe I've thought of a plan to pacify the crew so that we can be together and –'

'Miles – I mean, Captain Nash,' Bronwyn interrupted, straightening her face after her earlier amusement. 'Please do not speak any further. There's something I need to say and it's very important I say it now.'

'I'm listening,' he replied, a frown weighing on his brow.

'Last night, it was... indescribable. I have never in my life felt pleasure quite like that.'

Miles smiled, but he missed nothing. The deepening of his frown made it clear he had correctly guessed that there was more to this speech than a showering of compliments.

'But I'm afraid what passed between us, well, it cannot happen again. I want you to know that I do not plan to marry Price when I return to St Davids. I believe what you have told me and I will not break off my engagement with Leonard until you have the treasure you want, and with it your revenge.'

'But you do not wish to be with a pirate...'

'Not one who kidnapped me.' Bronwyn almost winced when she saw the pain in Miles's eyes. But even though he was kind, tender even at heart, there was no escaping what he had done or the consquences of his actions.

She put her hands on her hips in a show of determination. 'I know I am... spirited and, at times, forward. But I am a respectable woman at heart. And after what happened to Alex, a life at sea would not be fitting for me in any case. Even with a man as distracting as you standing by my side.'

'You need not say any more,' said Nash. 'It was presumptious of me to assume that just because we... that you would want something more permanent with a man in my... profession.'

'Perhaps, just a little bit presumptuous,' Bronwyn said with half a smile that did little to lighten the mood between them. 'But given my behaviour last night you can hardly be blamed for drawing the conclusions you did.'

He looked deep into her eyes and, when he spoke, his voice was laced with so much pain it cut straight through her. 'Is there no way at all of me redeeming myself in your eyes?'

Bronwyn opened her mouth to answer but then thought better of it. The truth was she wanted nothing more than to take this wretched man into her arms right now. Cecily's tragic mistake was to choose another man over Nash who would have taken care of her every need and ensured she was forever safe from the ills of the world. She knew she was making the same mistake but if she told him she had doubts; that there was a small part of her that believed he might be able to earn her forgiveness over the kidnapping, it would be giving false hope. For regardless of her feelings, she had no intention to wed him.

'No, Nash,' she said with a small shake of her head. 'I'm afraid there isn't.'

His amber eyes lowered and without looking at her again he nodded. Not wishing to witness the hurt her words had inflicted, Bronwyn turned and walked back to the quarter deck. Doing all she could to hold back tears as she went.

CHAPTER FOURTEEN

ast ahoy!' James bellowed down to deck.

Miles, who had spent the vast majority of the afternoon in his quarters doing what he could to overcome the embarrassment he felt at overstepping with Bronwyn, let out a heavy sigh. Couldn't a pirate kidnap a woman for thirty days in peace? Wasn't the ocean broad and deep enough to go a month without seeing another ship?

Apparently nay.

He winced instinctively as he stood from his desk, littered with navigational charts, and stalked towards the door. He had barely healed from the battle he had unwillingly fought not three days ago. He did not relish the thought that he might have to fight again so soon.

The bracing sea air hit him at once as he strode onto the deck, walked to the bow of the ship and lifted his spyglass.

Another boat was heading their way.

And not just any ship. It was a Ship of the Line, much bigger than Miles's galleon and undoubtedly packing a lot more fire power.

'Is it trouble?' Bronwyn asked. She must have sidled up behind him while he was making his assessment of the incoming vessel.

'I'm not sure,' he said, making sure to keep his tone neutral. He had wondered, more than once, that afternoon if it had been a mistake sharing his somewhat risqué desires with her this morning. She hadn't seemed outraged, more amused, but she had spurned him soon after. She even admitted he had been presumptuous with his designs on her. It was best to keep a safe and measured distance to reassure her he had understood her terms of engagement.

Again, he raised the spyglass. Something was inching up the mast of the ship – a white flag! Though there would likely be a great deal of treasure for the taking on a ship of that size, they would be imprudent to at least parlay with the crew first given they were significantly outgunned. Miles would much rather avoid the ship altogether but it was unlikely his crew would keep him in post as captain if he didn't at least explore the possibility of greater riches.

'Their advancing fast on us Cap'n,' said Rookwood. 'Regardless of their flag, best to have the men at the cannons, just in case.'

'Aye,' Miles said with a nod. 'Let's not leave anything to chance.'

'Hmmm,' Rookwood said, taking another look at the ship. 'The crew member stood at the bow, I think he might be Price's right-hand man.'

'Medlyn,' said Bronwyn. 'Leonard must have sent him. He's here to make the exchange early. That must be it... May I, Mr Rookwood?'

On realising Bronwyn wanted to use his spyglass Rookwood almost grimaced but managed to keep his composure long enough to hand the woman his glass. As she lifted it to her eye, Miles couldn't help but stare at her. The scarred side of her face was nearest him and looking at it up close again he was almost overcome with the desire to take her into his arms and kiss that labyrinth of red scorings across her otherwise perfect flesh. Nobody would care for this woman the way he would.

She did not plan to marry Price, that was at least some comfort, but if Medlyn was here to make the trade and take her back to Wales so soon and they had taken the trouble to track down his ship, then Price must be keen. Perhaps Miles had underestimated the man and he had fallen hard for the girl. He knew himself how beguiling a presence she had.

But no, Miles knew Price too well.

If he really had some mission to marry her, he probably wouldn't allow a little thing like her consent stand in the way. Who knows if he would accept Bronwyn's wishes to not be wed? And once they were married, how long would it be before he tired of her? Just as he had Cecily. He had failed to save one woman. He wasn't sure how he would save this one. He only knew that he must not fail again.

The approaching ship drew close enough for Miles to see there was no mistake, Medlyn was on board. The only small mercy was that there was no sign of Price.

'Permission to come aboard to parlay, captain,' Medlyn called through cupped hands.

Miles paused. If he agreed to this Bronwyn would be gone forever. The plan that he had hatched last night was to return to St Davids, take the treasure to appease the crew and steal Bronwyn away with him too as an extra punishment to Price for his sins. But there was no chance of that now. If he had wanted to, Medlyn could have blown them clear out of the water.

'Granted,' Miles called back, hoping that a conversation with Medlyn would at least give him time to think of a way to keep Bronwyn by his side. 'But only you may board.'

With a nod, Medlyn ordered his crew to move the two ships closer. Grappling hooks and ropes were thrown over the side of The Serpent. Then a plank was laid for Medlyn to navigate the now negligible distance between their vessels.

'You look in good health, Miss Rees,' Medlyn said to Bronwyn once he was on board. Though his words were civil, he spoke with an unmistakable sneer. Miles had met this type of man servant before. Utterly adoring of their masters to the point that they showed others nothing but disdain. He likely thought Bronwyn beneath Price and didn't appreciate his master handing over such a considerable portion of his wealth to a pirate for her return.

'Is there somewhere quiet we can talk, Captain? The lady should be present too of course, since this business concerns her.'

Miles shot Rookwood a look that he required no help in interpreting. If any of Medlyn's crew even looked at them the wrong way while they were in parlay, Miles wanted them taken out, no matter how many guns they had on their side.

'My quarters are this way,' Miles said, gesturing towards the stern. Medlyn started walking, as directed, towards the rear of the boat and Bronwyn followed.

Striding behind them, Miles's stomach began to churn. If he didn't think of a plan post haste, he would soon be saying goodbye to Bronwyn forever.

CHAPTER FIFTEEN

'Won't you take a seat, Mr Medlyn,' Miles asked, gesturing to a chair.

'I will remain standing, if you don't mind,' Medlyn said, looking down his nose at the chairs around the captain's table.

Bronwyn bristled. The snooty bag of bones probably thought he was too good to sit at a pirate's table when in truth Miles was ten times the man Medlyn would ever be. Bronwyn pulled out a chair and seated herself, just as Dodger came snuffling along looking for some fuss. She teased his soft brown ears between her fingers and only then, when petting the mutt brought her some relief, did she realise her shoulders were so tightly clenched. Why? Should she not see Medlyn's arrival as a welcome release from her captivity? Should she not be glad of safe passage home, away from the ocean and this ship and... the pirate?

Bronwyn swallowed hard. She had beseeched Miles so passionately to return home just two days ago, and had been furious at him for denying her. But now the moment was here, and the thought of never again seeing those amber eyes burning as they raked over her body left her with the emptiest of sensations in her stomach.

'I will get to the point,' said Medlyn. 'No sense in enduring these… conditions any longer than necessary.'

Miles eyed the man, glanced at Bronwyn and then returned his gaze to Price's underling.

'It comes to this. I have been dispatched by my employer to inform you, you may do with this girl as you wish.' A satisfied grin spread across Medlyn's thin lips. 'The Master has no intention of handing you even a piece of gold for her return.'

Miles's brows raised in surprise. 'Has your master forgotten the consequences of not paying his debt to me?' he growled.

'Lord Price has put contingencies in place to ensure you, and your pitiful band of cutthroats, are no threat to Pembroke. Certain coastal security measures that you have no hope of evading. My master favours the younger less-blemished sister, always has. And now that the elder, who has inherited the granite mines, has been woefully disappeared after being kidnapped by pirates, he shall be marrying her younger sister at the first opportunity and making the most of her inheritance.'

'Gwenllian,' Bronwyn gasped. 'But she won't agree to marry Price. Not after he failed to pay for my return.'

Medlyn feigned a grotesque look of remorse. 'Oh, but he tried. He sent me to the pirate to offer all of his treasure. I begged the merciless Captain Miles Nash to release her but the pirate had taken a liking to the wench and wouldn't honour his word. Instead, he tried to kill us and steal the treasure. We only escaped with our lives due to our many guns. Knowing that Bronwyn would rather die than be in the hands of pirates, we sank the ship and fear none survived.'

Bronwyn's eyes widened as she listened to the tale Medlyn and Price had created between them. Price was still well thought of back in Pembroke, there would be no reason for anyone to doubt their story. And right now she had no way to send a message and warn Gwenllian of Price's true motives. It was clear now he had wanted nothing more than to inherit their lucrative family granite mine and bleed her dry of any related money with his expensive tastes. All the while keeping his own considerable fortune intact.

Miles had begun to flex his fists. A flash of bloodthirsty malice burned in his eyes, deadlier than any threatening look he had given Bronwyn during the kidnap.

Oblivious to just how close Miles was to breaking point, Medlyn glanced pityingly at Bronwyn. 'Now, don't tell me this is a surprise to you. You didn't really believe the past few days that the master was going to hand over his family treasure for an ugly, scarred little thing like you, did you? You must have known that he couldn't care for a person who looked as you do. Your family business really was the only reason a man of my lord's status would ever consider such a match.'

Before Bronwyn could even blink, Miles had sprung and, gripping his hands tight around Medlyn's throat, had thrown him down on the table, pinning him in place. 'I hope you enjoyed the voyage here, Medlyn,' Miles hissed, 'because after that speech it's the last one you're ever going to make.'

Bronwyn rushed to his side and tugged at his arm, fearing she was about to witness a murder. 'Miles, please don't. He's not worth it.' In truth, Medlyn's words had not even scratched the armour she had built over the years since the fire. She had endured the horrified looks, paranoid whispers and direct insults over her appearance for years. Such slights could not touch her. But Medlyn's words seemed to have sent Miles into an immediate fury.

'On the contrary,' Miles said through gritted teeth. 'I think it's always worth teaching people like him some manners.' With this, Miles squeezed Medlyn's throat harder, causing him to writhe, desperate for air.

'You are better than murder, are you not?' Bronwyn said, trying to keep her voice calm in an attempt to appeal to Miles's finer feelings. Despite his choice to turn to piracy, she knew he had them. Miles turned his head to look at her then released his grip enough to let Medlyn talk.

'If you are going to sink my ship anyway, why should I let you go?'

'Because,' Medlyn croaked. 'I'm going to give you a chance to sail away freely. Price and I agreed that if you gave your word to never return to Pembroke, I should not sink your ship but merely tell everyone back in Wales that I did. But if you kill me, if I am not back out on that deck in thirty seconds, my crew have strict instructions to blow your ship to pieces and leave you for dead. If I were you, Captain, I would follow your lady's advice and let me go. You have a chance to live another day.'

Bronwyn watched as Miles contemplated Medlyn's words before slowly releasing his grip completely. 'Get off my ship. And don't you dare even look at the lady, let alone speak to her.'

Medlyn manoeuvred to his feet and then recovered himself enough to issue one last sly smile. 'How about that, it seems our foolish story about the pirate taking a liking to the wench wasn't far off the mark. You had better escort me back to my ship, Captain. I wouldn't want any of your crew asking me awkward questions about treasure.'

Miles gave one last glance to Bronwyn before following Medlyn out onto the deck, practically taking the door off its hinges as he slammed it behind him.

The second she was alone, Bronwyn covered her mouth and shook her head over all that had just taken place. She would be killed if she ever went home to Pembroke. Gwenllian would think her dead and was about to be coerced into marrying a villain. Bronwyn had no money, at least not with her. No passage back to Wales. No way of helping her sister. Tears stung her eyes as she looked out of the porthole at the endless blue beyond and wondered what on earth she was going to do.

CHAPTER SIXTEEN

When Miles returned to his quarters, Bronwyn was staring out of the porthole as though caught in some kind of trance. Her back was turned to him but he could tell from her posture that she was rigid with anger... or perhaps fear. Despite what she had said to him that morning, and after the callous words of Price's minion, he couldn't bear not to offer her a soothing, gentle touch. He reached out his hand to run his fingers through her silken hair. Before his fingers met their mark however, she began pacing up and down, wringing her hands as she went.

'Well, Captain, what's going to happen to me now?' she asked. 'What are you going to do with me?'

'What do you mean?'

'Now that my fiancé – I mean former fiancé – refuses to pay for my freedom, I remain your captive. My fate rests in your hands. So, I ask you, what are you going to do with me? I am not worth anything to you now.'

'You talk as if I am as heartless a monster as the man you were due to wed,' Miles said, struggling to hold his temper. He knew the lady had been through much but his fists clenched at her insinuation that she was worth nothing more than gold to him. Had he not tried to show her there was more to their relationship than that? She had said there was no hope of being forgiven for kidnapping her but he had hoped to at least make her think twice about that. Now he could see any attempts to win her affections had been in vain.

'I never said any such thing,' Bronwyn said, adopting the same petulant look she'd used when she sat at his dinner table the first night she was on board. His hands itched to throw her over his knee for a spanking. Though, he admitted privately, that desire had little to do with how irksome she was being.

'You may not have said it with your words. But your tone tells me everything I need to know.'

'All I did was ask a simple question,' said Bronwyn. 'My sister is in danger. I have no way of helping her and if it weren't for you I wouldn't be in this predicament.'

'If it weren't for me you would have already married Price yourself. I saved you from that fate, or have you forgotten?'

'Oh yes, your intentions were so selfless, so noble.'

Miles narrowed his eyes at her. He knew she was lashing out because she was scared but she was hitting nerves she had no business hitting given all he had tried to do to make amends. She wanted a pirate? Very well, she would get one.

'When you first boarded my ship I thought you intelligent. I am beginning to change my assessment.'

Bronwyn looked mildly outraged. 'Are you saying you think me a fool?'

'Yes, I am. You expect people to be perfect. God himself does not ask that. Even he permits us to repent. But not you.' Miles took a deliberate step towards her and stared into her eyes. 'Yes, I did kidnap you in an attempt to give Price what he deserved. And yes, in retrospect I can see that my plan was not without its consequences. But I have done other things besides kidnap you. I also comforted you. Listened to you. Respected you. Saved your life and, in your own words, given you a pleasure the likes of which you have never experienced before. People aren't just one act, Bronwyn, and you are not judge and juror. Only God has the right to judge me.'

'Are you suggesting that I just forget the trifling detail of my kidnap? All is forgiven?'

'No,' Miles said letting out a deep sigh in a bid to channel some of his frustration. 'What you think is no longer my concern. You could have been merciful but you chose not to be. We are a mere three miles from La Rochelle. We will dock there to replenish our supplies. I will pay some other sailor your passage back to Wales and then, *Princess*, I will have paid my debt to you and you will never see me again.'

'Good!' Bronwyn said, though tears watered in her eyes and he almost winced at the mere sight of them. 'Just so we're clear, as far as I'm concerned, you have done nothing for me. If I were not on this ship my life would not need saving and I would never have sought comfort in your arms. You say you saved me from marrying Price, that much may be true, but if it meant that my sister would be kept from harm I would have married Price one hundred times over. I never much cared what happened to me. My promise to my mother was to keep Gwenllian safe and now, because of you, I am in danger of breaking a promise to my mother for the first time in my life. And after all of this you will walk away with nothing. No treasure. No revenge. No hope with me.'

'Don't flatter yourself. I wouldn't take you now if you begged,' Miles ground out, just as the ship shook violently and a cataclysmic boom filled their ears.

CHAPTER SEVENTEEN

Despite the cutting slanders they had just thrown at each other, when the ship shook so violently, Miles grabbed Bronwyn and held her close, instinctively, protectively. She wanted to hate him after all his hurtful words but she couldn't. In part because he was right. He had done much to make amends for the kidnapping. Offered her comforts that no other pirate captain would have in his place. And she had remained determined to judge him; to push him away rather than give him a chance of redemption. She realised now, as she clung to his shirt and his strong arms held her steady, that she had done all this because she he was falling in love with him. And no truth scared her so much as that one did.

She had started falling for him during her first night on board when he had cradled her so tenderly in the night to keep her warm. She had bitterly missed such doting affection but giving her heart to another man after losing the first and now being betrayed by a second was a truly frightening prospect. If she opened her heart to a man like Miles she knew she would love him without any conditions or limitations. And when she lost him, which given the average life expectancy of a pirate was quite likely, there would be nothing left of her. There was barely anything left after Alex. She simply didn't have the resources to recover from a blow like that again, and yet she could not pull herself from his embrace.

Instead, she followed him out of the cabin door, her hand in his hand as Dodger yipped and circled their feet.

The moment they stepped outside Bronwyn's mouth fell open. Black smoke billowed from the deck.

'Medlyn,' Miles ground out. 'That back-stabbing scrub.'

Bronwyn's stomach churned. Was it her imagination or was the ship not quite listing. It seemed distinctly lower at the bow.

Before she could verify her suspicions, there were several more earth-shattering booms and with each bang the ship shuddered and groaned. 'He's going to sink us anyway,' she said, shaking her head. She had shown mercy to Medlyn, encouraging Miles to spare his life, and now they were all going to die.

'Is it a double-cross, Captain?' Rookwood asked, clinging to the nearby mast.

'Aye,' said Miles. 'I should have known. What's the word from the hull?'

'We're taking on water, Captain, and from the angle we're pointed at I'd say The Serpent'll be at the bottom of the ocean within the next quarter hour.'

Another boom sounded out and the whole boat lurched to starboard. Bronwyn threw her arms around Miles's waist to stop herself from being thrown overboard. His grip on her tightened and that much at least made her feel safe.

'Perhaps even sooner,' Rookwood corrected himself.

Miles shook his head. 'That's it then. Tell the men to grab what they can and abandon ship. We're roughly three miles off the coast of La Rochelle. We'll fit as many as we can into the jolly boat and tow everyone else to land. We'll need plenty of rope to make sure everyone's accounted for.'

'Aye, Captain,' said Rookwood and marched off to inform the crew of their orders.

'Lower the jolly boat!' Miles yelled. But no sooner had he shouted this than several cannonballs flew past the jolly boat, followed by three more that hit the small wooden skiff and reduced it to splinters.

Bronwyn gasped. There was no mistaking that they were sinking now. The drop between the side of the boat and the water below was less than half what it had been when Bronwyn had misguidedly thrown herself into the Atlantic. Water flooding from the hull was starting to flow along the deck. Crew members dashed from place to place, collecting rope, retrieving gold from their cabins and guzzling from rum bottles. That last behaviour struck Bronwyn as rather odd but then, she realised, they were probably hoping the drink would take the edge off just how cold the water was.

Bronwyn remembered how the water had turned her very blood to ice and shivered at the thought.

Just when she assumed things couldn't get any worse Mr Roberts approached with a murderous look on his face.

'You're no captain,' he barked at Miles, gesturing at the chaos that had broken out. 'Look at the mess you've made of us all,' he pointed an accusing finger at Bronwyn, 'over 'er.'

'Cheer up Roberts,' Miles said, mockingly. 'I'll likely be fish food at the end of all this and then you won't have to think of me anymore.'

'I'll make sure of it,' Roberts snapped, turning his back on Miles. Bronwyn thought that was the end of the matter but in truth Roberts had only turned himself about in search of a weapon. When he whipped around to face them again, he was brandishing a large lump of wood that looked as though it had once been part of the steering column. He swung at Miles's head before either of them could blink and scored a direct hit. At first Bronwyn was convinced the blow hadn't fazed Miles, for he didn't move. It was only a moment later that she realised his grip on her was loosening and his balance had deserted him and before she could even attempt to steady him, he fell clear from the deck and splashed into the ever-rising waters. 'Miles!'

Bronwyn screamed after him. While Dodger pounced on Roberts and dug his teeth into his leg.

Taking a deep breath, Bronwyn jumped from the now almost perpendicular deck into the ocean. It was as cold as she remembered but she didn't care. Miles was unconscious, and sinking. Submerging herself underwater, and trying to ignore the weight of her petticoats, she peered through the murky gloom this way and that. Searching for her black-shirted pirate with the sandy hair. After a moment she spotted him. He was so much deeper underwater than she had hoped. But she grabbed one of his hands and pulled with all her might. Using her free hand to drive them back towards the surface. Her lungs burnt under the strain of dragging Miles's body. His rounded stomach had seemed irresistibly soft when he had lain naked before her in front of the fire but it made manoeuvring him quite the task.

At last Bronwyn burst through the surface and did what she could to get Miles's head above water. She gasped as she saw that twenty feet away The Serpent's stern protruded just above water. The rest of the vessel was submerged and several of the crew thrashed around trying to gain purchase, gasping and yelling, reaching for something to cling to.

'Dodger!' Bronwyn called. Praying that the mutt had jumped from the vessel before it sank. 'Dodger!' she called, again and again. She saw no sign of the dog but then she heard a splashing to her left and there he was, paddling towards her with impressive speed. 'Oh Dodger, oh good boy,' she said.

'My lady.' Rookwood's familiar voice called from behind them. 'Over here.'

Bronwyn turned to see that Rookwood was perched upon a large piece of driftwood from the ship. And, most importantly, he held an oar. Jimmy was huddled next to him, shaking. She wasn't entirely sure whether to trust the men but, given that she could hardly pull Miles all the way back to La Rochelle by herself, she had little choice.

With what strength she had left she pulled Miles over to Rookwood's makeshift raft. She and Rookwood managed to drag Miles out of the water but when she tried to climb up alongside him the wood would not carry any more weight.

'Here,' Rookwood said, throwing Bronwyn some rope. 'I will row us back to La Rochelle as best I can. The ocean is calmer than yesterday so we've got a good chance of making it. Tie that rope around your waist and I'll get Jimmy here to hold onto you. Three miles is a long way to swim.'

Treading water, Bronwyn did as Rookwood instructed and tied the rope around her waist.

'Is Miles alive?' she asked, casting a worried glance at his body sprawled out on the make-shift raft.

Rookwood held the back of his hand near Miles's mouth. 'Aye, he's still breathing. It looks like you saved his life, just as he saved yours.'

Bronwyn nodded her approval, relief surging through her, and began to swim in small strokes towards a brown strip she could see on the horizon. Dodger splashed about next to her and she was glad of his company. Like Rookwood said, three miles was a long way to swim.

CHAPTER EIGHTEEN

iles had spent the last hour frantically searching for Bronwyn by the dockside in the afternoon heat of La Rochelle. He was still weak from the blow Roberts had dealt him but was doing all he could to ignore the occasional dizziness that threatened to overcome him. He should have known Roberts's greed would lead him to such an action. Not content with the extra share of loot he received for his duties as quartermaster, Roberts was forever pestering Miles about what his plans were for taking yet more riches. With the promise of Price's treasure, the rest of the crew were content to take the odd vessel to keep themselves in food, whores and rum. But not Roberts. He was never sated. The only reason Miles hadn't paid more attention to what he was up to as The Serpent sank was because he was too concerned with Bronwyn's safety.

And now she was lost too.

As he had first begun rouse at the harbour in the shadow of the city's spires and domes, the vague outline of her face had floated over him. By the time he had regained strength enough to stand, however, she had taken her leave to search for passage back to Wales. Hoping to find someone in one of the dockside drinking establishments heading to Britain who was happy to receive payment at the end of the trip.

With most of the crew now lost or dispersed, and it being more than clear that Price wasn't going to exchange her for any riches, Rookwood had seen no cause for holding her. Apparently, he'd had to heavily restrain Dodger from following her.

That fickle, flea-bitten excuse for a hound!

The ale houses of La Rochelle were not known to be the safest place for a woman to venture alone. It was a great relief then, when he spotted her blonde head step out of one of the drinking houses. Side-stepping around some drunken oafs soaking up the sun near the doorway. She turned away from Miles, clearly not having noticed him and so he set off after her at a run. He had only gone a few paces however, when he saw a dark figure emerge from the side of one of the buildings. There was something familiar about the way the figure moved. Whoever it was, he grabbed Bronwyn by the hair and dragged her out of sight. An action that at once spurred Miles onward despite his considerable fatigue.

Miles had only his dagger left after the sinking. His long sword had been lost when he fell into the ocean. Still, he had his fists and perhaps his height and breadth would be enough to scare off whoever it was anyway. How unprepared he was for such a confrontation of course, didn't matter. Bronwyn was in trouble. That was the only fact of consequence.

As quickly as he could with what strength he had, Miles sped towards the gap between the ramshackle buildings, through which Bronwyn had been stolen. What he found when he rounded the corner made every muscle he had tense in fury.

Roberts.

That sickly worm had survived the sinking somehow. And must have been watching them from a safe distance since he washed up. He'd have thought himself the luckiest bastard on earth when Bronwyn wandered off alone. Miles dreaded to think how Roberts might debase the woman he felt belonged to him. Just as he belonged to her.

Roberts had Bronwyn pinned up against the wall with a knife to her throat.

'When I'm done with you there'll be nothing left of you,' he spat. 'I'm going to have a jolly old time with you my girl. And you'll be taking some payback for what you did to my hand too.'

Bronwyn did not respond. True to form, she wasn't crying or begging, just watching her attacker closely, likely trying to think up some means of escape. Miles was only too happy to help her in that capacity.

Drawing his dagger, he stole up on Roberts. Inch by inch he crept closer. Holding his breath so that he didn't make a sound as he approached. He had let Roberts off with a mild choking last time he'd touched Bronwyn. This time, he would make sure he did not come back for more. Without a moment's hesitation, Miles raised his arm, poised to strike and then thrust the dagger hard into Roberts's side, all the way to the hilt. Blood pooled around the blade at once. Miles could feel his own breath almost quivering out of him at the sight.

Unlike many other members of his crew, who would no doubt revel in maiming someone who had wronged them as badly as Roberts had wronged him, Miles took no satisfaction in it. Bronwyn had stopped him killing Medlyn and would no doubt disapprove of him dispatching Roberts, but he was doing what had to be done. Roberts had brought this on himself.

The depraved trickster groaned out and reeled at the attack. He waved the knife in his hand around blindly, trying to manage the excruciating pain and defend himself at the same time. Miles withdrew his knife and would have stabbed him again but Bronwyn grabbed his arm.

'That's enough,' she said, and duly, Miles lowered his blood-stained weapon.

Roberts stumbled backwards. Clutching his wound, he groaned until he at last fell to his knees.

'You shouldn't see this,' Miles said, trying to turn her away.

But she brushed his hand from her shoulder and watched Roberts fall sideways, unable to hold himself upright a moment longer. She stared on, not even blinking as he lay, writhing on the ground. His breathing became shallower and shallower until at last his chest rose and fell no more.

It was only then Bronwyn looked away and fixed her eyes on Miles. He could not read her expression.

'I had to,' he said. 'We could not have a man like that on our trail.'

'I know,' she replied. 'He tried to kill you, and probably would have killed me too after he was done with me. Or worse, sold me on to someone else.'

'I would never have let that happen.'

She looked up at him with her stormy blue eyes and he was about to lean in and take her into his arms when she took a deep breath and walked past him.

'I am no longer your concern, Captain Nash,' she said as she marched back towards the waterfront.

CHAPTER NINETEEN

Bronwyn took several deep breaths – in and out – as she looked over the harbour of La Rochelle. The sun was high in the sky and something about that made her feel quite sick. That the sun could shine so passionately in the sky while she was on the ground being mauled by a foul-smelling, murderous lout, and then had watched as he died. And that was after a three-mile swim in an ocean so deathly cold she still couldn't feel her hands.

Though she had tried to brush him off, she knew Miles was approaching. She couldn't say exactly how she knew. Her skin tingled with the sense that he was near, and sure enough a moment later he appeared in her peripheral vision.

'I've just saved your life,' he said.

She turned to face him. 'I've just saved your life.'

This gave Miles pause, but only for a moment. 'I saved your life twice.'

'Do you have a point, Captain?' Bronwyn said, putting her hands on her hips.

'I saved your life twice because…' he looked out to sea as though he would find the reason in the gentle swell then turned his amber eyes back on her. 'I care for you.'

Bronwyn was unsure what to say to this. She should just admit that she cared for him too, of course. That would be the most straightforward thing to do. But she knew where it would lead. To being in his arms. To her forgetting everything and everyone else. And she couldn't afford to do that right now.

'My priority is my sister,' Bronwyn said. 'I must get back to Wales and stop her wedding to Price. Not to mention letting her know her sister is still alive so she is not alone in the world. Besides anything else, I assumed after all that was said on The Serpent, and given that you cannot barter me for treasure, that you would have preferred me gone when you came round,' said Bronwyn, and, of course, if it weren't for her, The Serpent might still be afloat. She had prevented Miles from dealing with Medlyn in his own way and it had cost him his ship. The ship on which he was going to sail away with his beloved Cecily. Bronwyn had expected Nash to be furious about that, and didn't feel like waiting around to find out just how fierce his anger might be.

'You assumed wrong,' said Miles, placing his hands on her shoulders. 'We both said things on the Serpent in anger.'

'I am not a fool, Miles. You meant what you said... and you were right. I should have given you a chance to redeem yourself.'

'Well, I didn't think it prudent to wait around for you to give me a chance to redeem myself so I just went ahead and did it anyway,' Miles said, a grin spreading across his lips.

Bronwyn looked at him side-long. 'What exactly do you mean by that?'

'I mean, Rookwood managed to save quite a lot of money from the ship before she went down. He has secured us passage on a ship headed to Liverpool. They will dock at St Davids for us to disembark.'

Bronwyn's eyes widened. 'Is this true?'

'It is... though I must confess it's not a completely selfless act. Me, Rookwood and Jimmy will be going after Price once we land. But

I insisted to Rookwood you should be granted passage too, and he has agreed.'

'I'm going home?' Bronwyn's eyes filled with tears and she grabbed Miles's arms, squeezing them in excitement. 'I'm really going home? When do we leave?'

'Aye,' Miles said, clearly moved by just how happy he had made her. 'Anchor's up an hour from now.'

'Oh, so soon. That's wonderful. Oh, thank you,' she said, and then flashed him an impish little smile. 'It's such a shame that I've already decided I wasn't going to be with a pirate like yourself. If I hadn't been so rash, I would have been able to kiss you as thanks for such a generous act.'

At her words, Miles's stare intensified. He grabbed her by the waist and pulled her into his body so that their faces were but an inch apart, his lips hovering over hers.

'I've always thought that it is a woman's prerogative to change her mind, haven't you?' he said, his eyes falling to her mouth.

'Well in that case, I've changed my mind, Miles,' she whispered. 'I want you to kiss me, and if it's not too much trouble, I'd like you to keep on kissing me for as long as it pleases you.'

Miles smiled and clinched her tighter. 'Oh Princess, those are bold words. I am going to want to kiss you for a very, very long time.'

At the sound of those words, an indescribable warmth spread through Bronwyn's chest. It was as though her heart was growing. Or perhaps it was healing. She had not thought it possible but perhaps with the devotion of a man like Miles, her heart could be whole again and she vowed right then to do everything in her power to glue the broken pieces of his heart back together too.

As he closed the gap between his mouth and hers, her eyes fluttered closed so she could concentrate only on the heat of his breath. On the way his lips swallowed her own so completely as she gently sucked on his tongue which tasted sweet and vaguely of rum. His hands roamed from her waist down to her rear and he drove his hips into her in such a way that she could feel his hardness through the fabric of her skirt. She moaned into his mouth to let him know just how exciting she found it that he wanted her so fiercely, and she received a groan full of yearning in return.

When their lips parted there was something smug about Miles's smile that put Bronwyn on edge. 'What aren't you telling me?'

'It's nothing,' Miles said, his grin widening. 'It's just Rookwood couldn't afford to pay for an individual cabin for everyone on the boat. So… we'll have to share.'

Biting her lip, Bronwyn stared into those eyes that seemed to be ablaze with want and did all she could to fight a smile.

CHAPTER TWENTY

Tentatively, Miles eased open the door to the cabin he and Bronwyn had been allocated. The Glory was a much bigger and more luxurious boat than The Serpent had ever been and the merchants who were transporting them back to Wales had seen fit to provide Bronwyn with a tub and enough boiled water to bathe in.

She was in there now. Completely nude. Only soap bubbles inhibited his view of her as he stood in the doorway. His eyes raked over her soft, freckled form. Over the most delicious curve where her neck met her back. Her shoulders seemed so delicate as she brought the sponge to them and squeezed. The sight of all that water flowing over her flesh drew a tortured groan from him. She whipped round at once at the sound. Her eyes wide until she confirmed it was him.

'Miles!' she shrieked, crossing her arms over her chest. 'You promised you'd make yourself absent.

'I thought you may want some help,' he said, walking towards the tub.

'I am perfectly capable of bathing myself, thank you Mr Nash.'

'I know you can bathe yourself, I just thought you might enjoy it more if I were to assist you.'

'Rather than bathing me, you should be focused on the plan for when we return to Pembroke. Are the others in agreement?'

'It is all settled. Rookwood and Jimmy were both impressed by your imaginative methods.'

'Well, you inspired the plan actually. You said it yourself, there is nothing Price loves more than his money. And yes, you could just steal the jewels as you originally intended but he'd just go on to acquire more wealth though some other manipulative means. Or see you in prison for his loss. If this works, however, we'll cut him off at the source and he'll be poor for the rest of his days.'

'If it doesn't work, Rookwood and Jimmy have refused to accept your dowry as compensation.'

'Oh but they must!' Bronwyn said, and then her eyes narrowed. 'You didn't intimidate them into refusing it, did you?'

Miles pressed a hand against his chest as though this was the most outrageous accusation he'd ever heard. But he made sure to accompany this gesture with a grin.

'Miles...'

'I didn't intimidate anyone,' he said with a chuckle. 'They wouldn't outright admit it but Rookwood and Jimmy admire you and even if they end up with no treasure out of this, after what Price did to The Serpent, seeing him so publicly humiliated for his crimes will be worth its weight in gold to them.'

'I can hardly wait to see the look on Price's face myself.'

'Captain Moyes says we should be in Pembroke tomorrow morning. Medlyn will have reported that our boat was sunk. They will think us either dead or stranded so will not have any reinforcements waiting for us. I think Price will press Gwenllian to marry him sooner rather than later but he will still, for propriety's sake, have to give her a few days to mourn your passing.

Which means we should be in ample time to put a stop to any wedding he might have arranged.'

'Good. Now let me have my bath in peace.'

'Oh, I see,' Miles said with a chuckle. 'I'm a disturber of your peace now, am I'

'I have had little peace since you first came into my life, shall we say that?'

'Sounds to me like I am in debt to you,' he said, gripping her wrists and slowly moving her crossed arms from her breasts. 'I have seen your body before and I will see it many times before this trip is over. You have no need to hide something so beautiful from me.'

Her breathing quickened as his eyes fixed on her body, which only made her breasts rise and fall in a more frantic manner. He remembered well how they had filled his mouth when he sucked on them. He looked forward to circling his tongue around those rose pink nipples again in the very near future. But for now, he must help her relax. Though she had said it in jest, it was true that she had not known any peace since he had carried her off to The Serpent. More than anything, he wanted to find ways to attend to this woman's every need. Therein lay redemption, and, he believed, the path to her heart.

'I'm scared,' she said, quite unexpectedly.

'Of me?'

'No... of everything. Of what might right now be happening to Gwenllian. Of whether we'll be able to save her. Of this...' she waved a hand between herself and Miles.

Slowly, he stroked her hair. 'You have only known me for a short time, but in that time I have protected you, have I not?'

Bronwyn nodded.

'And I will continue to do so with every ounce of strength I have in me,' he said. 'As for what we share, you have no reason to be afraid of it.'

'But what will happen, after you get your revenge on Price? You will sail away and I will never see you again.'

Miles had to work hard to keep his surprise from reaching his face, but he just about managed it. After all they had been through, did she really believe he would just abandon her once his revenge was complete?

'Bronwyn, do you think I give myself lightly to a woman?'

She thought for a moment before answering and then the smile he had been hoping to see crept over her lips. 'No.'

'When we have made sure Price gets what he deserves, the only place I will be sailing is into your arms. You were right to be hesitant about our tryst. A woman like yourself should not be matched with a pirate. Which is why I intend to restart my shipping business in Pembroke and work my way up to being respectable again. Well, as respectable as an American could ever hope to be seen in the old country.'

'You're going to do that, for me?'

'Do you remember when you told me there was nothing I could do to earn your forgiveness?'

'Yes,' Bronwyn said, her head dipping in shame.

'I didn't believe you. Because I knew I was willing to do whatever it took to make you see me as I truly am, rather than what I let Price turn me into.'

'I do see you as you are,' she said, leaning close enough to run her fingers over his lips and through his hair. 'I forgive you.'

At those three little words, Miles could barely contain his elation. He drew her hand to his mouth and kissed it, pressing his lips to every finger, knowing that he would spend the rest of the night showing her that she had made the right choice to trust him.

'Lay back,' he said. 'And let me wash your hair.'

Without hesitation, she did as he instructed. For his part, Miles drew up a chair, worked up a lather with the soap and then began slowly massaging her head. With every circle of his fingers her tender body seemed to relax just that little bit more. Small, contented moans escaped her lips as he continued to rub along her hairline and as she lay there, he thought about all of the exquisite noises he would hear from that mouth between now and dawn.

CHAPTER TWENTY-ONE

If it was possible to glow inside and out, then Bronwyn was sure that was precisely what was happening to her as she curled up in the cot just big enough for two. The door opened and a cool breeze blew in as Miles returned from his last check-in with Captain Moyes for the night. For one so keen to earn her trust, Miles was not greatly trusting of others and had checked the ship's course and progress several times since their boarding.

As soon as he closed the door however, a rakish smile overtook him and he hurried to the bed.

Pulling back the blanket, he raised an eyebrow. 'You're wearing your shift.'

It took all of Bronwyn's might not to laugh at his disappointment that she was at least part clothed again after her bath, but she managed to contain herself. 'Only so you can rip it off me, Captain.'

At her words, Miles seemed to go into some kind of trance. His jaw slackened and his eyes widened. She smiled demurely, he had nigh on suggested they copulate in front of his crew back on The Serpent. But, it seemed, he didn't expect such forward suggestions from her. If that was the case, he was in for a few surprises.

'Technically, I'm no longer a captain as I have no ship,' he said, when he at last found his voice.

'You are my captain,' she replied, luxuriating in the light trapped in those amber eyes. 'Now, undress, so I can look at every part of my captain.'

He didn't require any further prompting. Keeping his eyes fixed on her, he at once yanked off his boots and pulled off his shirt. The wound he had sustained was healing much better now and required a smaller bandage. Bronwyn took in the sight of his chest. A significant covering of dark hair ran all the way down to his navel. As she stared at him, she could feel her body responding to his. She knew how soft that hair was to the touch. She wanted to stroke it.

Next, Miles unhooked his belt and let his breeches fall to the floor. She gasped as she took in the full view of his naked body before her. She had seen him unclothed before of course, but it hadn't been at an angle by which she could take in the full spectacle. His arms and thighs were so firm. The muscles toned from many months at sea. His rounded tummy was somehow all the more alluring for its contrast with the other parts of his body. And there was no missing his sizeable pole. For it stood proud of him by some inches and right now it was hard and bulging.

'If I climb into bed with you, the chances of me stopping until we are both fully sated are small. Are you sure you want this?'

'I've never been surer of anything,' she said, with a little frown. 'Why would you need to stop?'

'For one, I had hoped to bed you for the first time in greater luxury than this,' he said, indicating the wooden cabin with a sweep of his hand. The fittings were of higher standards than those on The Serpent but still not what one might call cosy. 'And for another, if we do this there is a chance of a child.'

Bronwyn had already thought of that, of course. Again she wanted to laugh at the way in which he presented this fact as though it might be new information to her, but he was trying to be considerate so laughing at him wasn't really good form. 'I don't care about the where, Miles. I want you and it is no more complicated than that. As for the potential consequences, I had assumed that if I bore you a child you would take care of us. Am I wrong to think that?'

Miles rushed into the bed and at once began tearing off her shift. 'No,' he murmured between desperate kisses. 'You are not wrong to think that. Oh I would take better care of you and the child than anyone has in your life. You would want for nothing.'

Tears filled Bronwyn's eyes, but she fought them back. She could tell from Miles's ardour that the thought of Bronwyn having his child was, for him, one of salvation. He would care for her and a child the way he would have cared for Cecily and hers. What surprised her was the incredible warmth that spread through her at the thought of bearing his child. Quite different to the dread that had surfaced whenever she'd thought of producing an heir for Price. With Miles she would be happy, and their child would be too.

Bronwyn's whole body arched as Miles parted her thighs and began exploring the area with his fingers.

'Oh... it seems you enjoyed watching me undress.'

'I did,' Bronwyn said, reaching her hand down to his rod, which was already moist at the tip. 'It seems you enjoyed undressing for me.'

As soon as her hands connected with his shaft, Miles began to groan and growl in time to the long strokes she was making up and down the length of him.

'Have you been taken before?' he asked.

'Once,' Bronwyn said. 'Before Alex went away.'

'So you know something of what to expect?'

'Yes,' Bronwyn said, kissing his jawline and rubbing the side of her head against his beard.

'I want you to get on top of me, Princess.'

'I've never done it that way,' Bronwyn said, suddenly quite nervous about making sure Miles had a good time here.

'Neither have I, but I have an idea that you will look...' he paused to cast his eyes over her shoulders and her breasts before once again meeting her eyes, 'spectacular. And don't worry.

CHAPTER TWENTY-ONE

My hands will guide you. I'll take us both where we want to go.'

Calmed somewhat by the fact that Miles saw this first encounter as a joint effort, Bronwyn manoeuvred herself on top of him, hovering just above. He took her hips in his hands and gently guided her downward, easing himself inside her inch by inch. Moans of desperation and craving escaped both their lips as he entered her. Their eyes were locked, and before long their bodies were too. Miles paused for a moment. Allowing her to adjust to him and seemingly memorising the view of her perched atop his body. Her every curve and crevice there for his private viewing.

His hands cupped her breasts, and squeezed. 'All the things I want to do with you...'

'I want to hear about them all,' Bronwyn said, instinctively thrusting her hips forward and gasping at the sensation of his pole pushing so deep inside her. Miles's eyes rolled back in his head for a moment, the feeling was one of such rapture. In response, Bronwyn began to work her hips in a steady rhythm, the same rhythm that she had used with her hands when she had stroked him.

'Oh, you look... so beautiful,' Miles said squeezing her breasts tighter. 'And you feel... oh... there aren't words for how you feel.'

'I need this,' she gasped back. 'I need you, Miles. I need you.'

Bronwyn wasn't quite sure what it was about these words that triggered such a striking response from him, but at once, Miles grabbed her buttocks in his hands, gripping her hips with his thumbs, and pushed himself even harder into her. His rod reached depths Bronwyn hadn't even thought possible and she arched her back in an attempt to drive her body even harder into his.

'Oh Miles! Don't stop...' she moaned, quickening her pace and almost bursting in ecstasy right there and then. He increased his speed too and held her in place as his hips rose and fell at a rate that felt almost animal. With every thrust she was sure his movements could get neither harder nor faster and yet he consistently proved her wrong, until she was bouncing up and down, back and forth with the sheer force of his body crashing against hers.

'I'm very close, Princess,' he growled. 'So very close...'

At these words, Bronwyn opened her legs even wider than before and rode him with nothing short of abandon, her body shaking and shuddering as she neared her peak. It was his orgasmic groans and the hard swell as he spilled his seed inside her that pushed her over the edge. She dug her nails into his chest as she climaxed and wailed in an almost feral manner before collapsing into his hairy torso. She was left panting hard from the intoxicating blend of exertion and excitement, but a moment later she smiled as his arms rose to encircle her.

CHAPTER TWENTY-TWO

The next morning Miles woke to the smell of coffee. He rolled over in the cot and saw Bronwyn setting two mugs down on a chair next to the bed.

'Damn,' he said. 'I was going to get you coffee this morning. How long have I slept?'

'It is eleven,' Bronwyn smiled. 'But I was happy to fetch the coffee. I had a chance to pet Dodger, he was begging breakfast off the crew when I went down. They are all quite enamoured with him.'

Miles shook his head. 'That dog would beg for crumbs after an eight course meal.'

Bronwyn chuckled but just as quickly her humour evaporated. 'Captain Moyes says the winds were not in our favour last night, though we will still reach Pembroke by two.'

Worry lines marked her forehead, and Miles tenderly reached a hand out to her chin. 'Fear not, we will be in time to stop any designs Price has on your sister. I'm sure.'

Bronwyn nodded and at least tried to smile.

'Come here,' he said opening his arms to her and then, when a cool draft blew under the blanket, remembered that unlike her he was still unclothed.

Bronwyn raised an eyebrow at his naked form, a gesture that at once sent the blood rushing through his veins.

She climbed into bed with him, rested her head on his arm and ran her fingers through his hair. He had barely recovered from the pleasure she had delivered to him last night. It had travelled to the end of every nerve and somewhere deep inside had branded him as hers. But laying with her now, lazily, contentedly, brought him even greater satisfaction. Nobody had touched him with such affection nor looked at him with such longing. He was safe to express who he truly was with her. He knew that.

'I am in love with you, Bronwyn.' The words were out of his mouth before he could stop them.

Bronwyn's eyes widened and for a moment he wished the words back into his mouth, but then she flashed her impish smile.

'Are you sure?' she said, teasingly.

'I am indeed,' he said, surprised by the rich humour in his own voice. She brought out his playfulness, something that he had lost what felt like forever ago. How he had missed finding the fun in quiet moments.

'I'll be the judge of that, what are your symptoms?'

'Well, you are my first thought on waking and the last before I sleep. I cannot help but find a way to touch you whenever you are in my presence. I have the strangest urge to both protect and defile you for all I'm worth. And most serious of all, I keep imagining a future full of you, and the family we would have.'

'Oh dear,' Bronwyn said. Her tone was still mocking but there was no missing the tears in her eyes. 'I have exactly the same symptoms as you. This doesn't mean I'm in love with you too, does it? In love with a pirate? Whatever will people think?'

Miles let out a deep laugh that shook his whole body. Slowly, his hands began to wander down her back until he reached her buttocks.

'You suffer the same symptoms as I?'

'Yes?'

'All of them?'

'Yes,' she replied her tone growing suspicious.

'Including the urge to defile me?'

'I thought that might be the first thing you asked,' Bronwyn said with a giggle.

'It's an important question, I think,' Miles said hitching up her petticoats and gliding a finger up her thigh until he hit her honeypot. 'Oh, but I think I have my answer.'

She continued to laugh as he climbed on top of her but the moment he began massaging her with his fingers, those giggles turned to moans.

'It's such a shame we didn't acknowledge our feelings sooner,' he said, pulling her breasts from her stay with his spare hand and giving each one a squeeze in turn.

'I really would have loved to have taken you at the stern of the ship, at night, with the rain lashing down on us, sea foam frothing all around.'

'But the crew…' she gasped in such a way that Miles could tell she was rather enjoying the idea.

'The crew would have seen nothing more than glimpses of your pale thighs, gripping my body as I pounded into you.'

As he said this, Miles teased her opening with his pole. To his surprise, she lifted her hips, coaxing him inside.

'Oh… Bronwyn,' he said, pushing deeper and deeper, 'they would have envied me as I took you like that. They would have been straining to see around my body. To catch a flash of your breast or the look of ecstasy on your face as I drove into you as hard and as fast as I could.'

'But what would they think of a woman who opened her legs to a pirate like that?'

He smiled. 'They would know you were hungry for me, that you had a craving only my prick could satisfy.'

'Oh… Miles… I'm very, very close,' she whimpered with a helpless look in her eyes that only made him increase his rhythm. His rod swelled at the thought she was revelling in his fancies as much as he was. That she would entertain his darkest wants. He steeled himself for his next words. Unsure if it would be taking the fantasy too far, and yet still hungry to see her reaction.

'Some of the men would have been touching themselves as they watched us. Imagining themselves in my place, something I would never allow. Though they could imagine all they wanted.'

Her response could not have been more delicious. This idea, it seemed, was simply too much for her. Bronwyn's whole body tensed and she screamed out over and over, so much that Miles put a hand over her mouth which in turn only seemed to satisfy her more. She lay there for a moment, gasping and whimpering before slowly recovering herself and staring up at him.

'You filthy pirate,' she said, with a flirtatious smirk. 'You love the idea of other men wanting what you have, don't you?'

'Yes...' Miles hissed as he pushed in and out of her, his pace quickening; his peak near.

'You want them to see my body shaking and hear my moans, so they know just what you can do to a woman, don't you?'

'Yes... I want them to see me mark you as mine,' Miles said, gritting his teeth, aware that he couldn't hold on for much longer if she kept talking like this.

She slipped her hands down to his bared buttocks and teased his rear entrance with her fingers. 'You want to make me into your own little whore, don't you?'

With this comment it seemed Bronwyn had beaten Miles at his own game as he couldn't muster any kind of comprehensible response to that last question. Every muscle he had clenched as he ground his hips frantically into hers and filled her with his seed. He managed to thrust hard into her twice more, holding onto that moment of all-consuming, unparalleled bliss before falling into her arms and resting his head on her chest.

'You… you are perfect,' he whispered, still trying to catch his breath.

'So are you,' she returned.

CHAPTER TWENTY-THREE

ook! There it is. Pembroke. Oh, I've never been so glad to see it in all my life.' Bronwyn pointed from the port bow of The Glory towards the approaching landmass. It was almost two in the afternoon and the hazy sunlight was hitting the rugged green of the cliffs in just the right way. They were mottled with yellow and purple where wildflowers had taken root, and behind the craggy lines of the coastal landscape was a vast blue sky that Bronwyn hoped promised happier days ahead. 'Can I borrow your spyglass?' Bronwyn said, tapping Miles on the shoulder and hopping up and down on the spot. 'I bet I can see our little cottage from this vantage point.'

Chuckling, he pulled his spyglass from his belt and handed it to her.

She raised it to her eyes and adjusted the lense. 'Yes! Yes! I can see the cottage, you're just going to love it. I can't wait to show you. I...' Her body stiffened. 'Oh... no.'

'What is it?' Miles said.

'There are people there. They are dressed in mourning. I think... I think it might be my funeral procession.'

'Let me see,' Miles said, taking the spyglass and lifting it to his eye. After a moment he slowly lowered the glass and looked back at her.

'They think me dead,' Bronwyn gasped. 'They really think me dead.'

'We knew that was inevitable,' said Miles. 'Medlyn had a ten hour lead on us and we knew what he would tell those you loved on his return. But the point is you are very much alive, Princess, and Price will soon be held accountable for putting both you and your family through this agony.'

Bronwyn felt tears stinging the backs of her eyes. Of course she had been prepared for the fact that Medlyn would tell everyone she was dead, but she hadn't expected to witness her own funeral. 'I should kill Price for this,' she spat out. 'This world would be better without him. It would be over quickly. Like it was for Roberts.'

'Bronwyn,' Miles said, swiping a single tear from her cheek. 'Don't talk of such things. Roberts wasn't going to stop coming after us.'

Bronwyn frowned. 'How do you know Price won't? Are you defending him now? After all he has done?'

'Leonard Price is a coward. He won't come after us after we're done with him. But no, I'm not defending him. You'd see pigs fly before you saw that. I'm defending you. Don't make the same mistake I did, love. Do not let Price win. If it hadn't been for you I'd still be walking that dark path right now. But you gave me a reason to let go of all that anger.'

'All of it?' Bronwyn said, narrowing her eyes.

Miles drew her into his arms, amused by her suspicious demeanor. 'I go after Price now for the sake of making him face up to the consequences of his actions, not bitter revenge. Your plan is fitting but it is tame in comparison to what some pirates would do to a person who crossed them the way Price crossed me. The truth is however, people like Price have black hearts, and if we let them blacken ours too, then they succeed in their task of making this world a more wretched place to live.'

Bronwyn took a deep breath. She knew Miles was right and part of her couldn't be prouder of him for taking such a high and moral stance when it came to the topic of Price. Miles had lost a lot to that man but he was willing to control himself in order to prove he was deserving of her love. As Bronwyn stared across to Pembroke however, squinting hard enough to see those little black dots moving along the cliff top, she wondered if she would be able to do the same. Price had tricked her, left her for dead, refused to rescue her, lied about what had happened to her and was at this moment planning to marry Gwenllian and ruin her too. In truth, a person could do all they want to her. Her armour was thick enough to endure it. But Lord help anyone who lay a finger on those Bronwyn loved. Taking a deep breath she tried with all her might to calm herself. They had a plan and Bronwyn would do her best to stick to it but the truth was, she had no idea what she might do when she next set eyes on Leonard Price.

CHAPTER TWENTY-FOUR

iles!' Bronwyn called from the front step of her little cottage. 'I believe it's safe to come in now.'

Miles pushed himself up from the wall he had been resting on and made his way to the front door. He had enjoyed staring at the cottage in the moonlight. The yellow glow of candles shining through the windows had set him off dreaming about what it would be like to live here with Bronwyn. The waves of St George's Channel crashed beyond the cliff edge not twenty feet away, which would always remind him of the strange way he and Bronwyn had met. He would re-start his shipping business and help her manage the granite mines. Their children would grow up with the sound of the ocean in their ears and perhaps even Bronwyn would learn to love those waters again. She had lost one love to the ocean but it had also brought love to her. He hoped one day she would scc it that way.

Bronwyn had, understandably, wanted to talk to her sister alone about all that had happened. From the small scream Miles heard shortly after Bronwyn had entered the cottage, Bronwyn's resurrection had come as something as a shock. Goodness knows how Gwenllian might have reacted if Bronwyn had entered with the pirate who kidnapped her in tow.

Miles stepped over into the threshold and was at once glad of the warmth. A fire was burning in the small reception room which was built of strong wooden beams. A table stood in the centre, where Miles briefly imagined his children sitting for an evening meal. Then he turned his attentions on Gwenllian who sat by the hearth in a rocking chair. Her eyes were a similar blue to Bronwyn's, though not as stormy as those of his beloved. Indeed Gwenllian had a much calmer manner about her over all, that was until she opened her mouth.

'Before you say a word, Mr Nash, you should know that I am outraged by your behaviour towards my sister.'

'My behaviour...' Miles floundered. It was past midnight. He had been on a long voyage. He thought Bronwyn had squared the past away with her sister. He had not been prepared for a confrontation.

'Kidnapping her the way you did, with a sword to her throat no less, and it seems to me you've managed to meddle with my sister's mind and trick her into holding affection for you. Well I won't have it.' Gwenllian stood up from the chair and crossed her arms.

Miles cringed when she brought up the kidnapping. Not exactly the best first impression to make on a woman he hoped would be his future sister-in-law.

'I – I – I never would have harmed Bronwyn. And I hope she has told you my reasons for the whole plot. Even if it was a misguided way of handling the matter, I treated her very well I assure you and...' Miles looked helplessly at Bronwyn. 'Did you tell the story right? Did you tell her the bit where I saved your life? Twice?'

Miles didn't get any further with his ramble because Bronwyn burst out laughing and Gwenllian followed her lead. The pair were in such hysterics they could barely stand upright.

Gwenllian was holding onto the back of the rocking chair for support while Bronwyn rested her hands on the sitting room table and even slapped her hand down on it a couple of times in case anyone in the room was confused about just how hilarious she found the situation.

'A bit of a cruel joke, don't you think?' Miles said with a disgruntled frown. But this only made the sisters laugh harder.

'Your face,' Gwenllian said through desperate hoots. 'Your face.'

On seeing just how unimpressed Miles was by the joke Bronwyn covered her mouth with a hand but it did little to smother her cackling.

'You sound like two old witches, the pair of you,' Miles said. He could hear the petulance in his voice but couldn't help himself.

'Ohhhh, I'm sorry, my love, come here,' Bronwyn said, walking over and wrapping her arms round him.

'I'm not sorry,' Gwenllian said, sobering up and pointing a finger at Miles. 'The joke was inappropriate, and so was kidnapping my Bronwyn and putting her life at risk. You do anything to hurt her again and you won't get off so lightly, understood?'

'Completely,' Miles said. 'I assure you, I wish nothing but your sister's happiness.'

Gwenllian narrowed her eyes at Miles a moment more, then offered a satisfied nod. 'Not that what I thought would matter much at any rate, given how Bronwyn's not stopped gushing about you since she walked in the door.'

'Gwenllian!' Bronwyn said, her cheeks burning. 'Don't exaggerate!'

Miles laughed. 'When this is all over I would like to hear more from you on that score, Gwenllian. But we had better start making arrangements for how we're going to deal with Price.'

'Gwenllian is due to marry him tomorrow afternoon,' Bronwyn said, now completely sobered up after their rouse.

Miles grimaced. 'So he gave you a whole day to mourn your lost sister, that's about as much compassion as I'd expect from him.'

'I didn't want to agree to marry him but, with Bronwyn gone and no suitable match in the village, I thought it was prudent. Now I see that nothing could be further from the truth. My sister tells me you have a plan to make sure Price gets all that's coming to him,' said Gwenllian. 'If it involves any kind of criminal charges I doubt they'll get very far. Even when he sank your boat and tried to kill you both, it all happened out at sea, and knowing how disgustingly devoted Medlyn is to him, he would probably claim his master knew nothing of his actions.'

'No, given his status, we don't expect to see him in the courts for any of this,' said Miles. 'But let's see how he responds when the ghosts of his past misdemeanours catch up with him, shall we?'

CHAPTER TWENTY-FIVE

he bride glided with effortless grace down the aisle of St Davids Cathedral, looking out at the congregation through her veil of white lace. After what had happened at the last wedding, there were fewer guests in attendance this time. Some, the bride had been told, were still nursing minor wounds after they had been attacked by a band of bloodthirsty cutthroats. But everyone of vital importance was present. Bishop Trevor, Leonard Price: Viscount of Pembroke, his father Charles Price: the Earl of Wrexham, Mr. Lothario Medlyn, several members of the village who considered themselves friends of the bride and of course, the bride herself.

She did not miss the smug look on Price's face as she strode purposefully to the altar. She could only hope the events that were about to unfold would wipe that look off his face for good. To her mind, he deserved a lot worse but Miles had been correct: the only way to hurt a man like Price was to take away his money, the one thing in the world he was in any way attached to.

'Dearly beloved,' Bishop Trevor began, 'we are gathered here in the presence of thy holy father to join in matrimony Gwenllian Alys Rees and Leonard Louis Price.'

The bride took a deep breath as Bishop Trevor turned to her. The sound of her heart thumping in her chest felt so loud she wondered how the others present couldn't hear it.

'Will you, Gwenllian Alys Rees, take this man as thy wedded husband?' said Bishop Trevor. 'Will you obey him, love him, and honour him, forsaking all others, so long as you both shall live?'

'No!' the bride shouted. 'I should rather die. Although, of course, according to Mr Price, I already have.'

Gasps rose from the small congregation as the bride removed her veil and turned to reveal herself as none other than Bronwyn Rees.

She shot a triumphant look at Price, whose face had turned utterly pale.

'B-B-B- Bronwyn?' Price sputtered, while Medlyn stood just behind his liege, his cheeks purple with fury and his fists clenched tight.

'Forgive the dramatic entrance,' said Bronwyn. 'But had I not come in disguise, I feared that my fiancé-that-was might try to kill me. Again.'

'What is the meaning of all this?' said the Earl of Wrexham, rising from his pew. 'We were told you were dead, Bronwyn.'

'I know my lord,' Bronwyn said, being sure to make eye contact with the Earl and offering a respectful bow of her head as she addressed him. 'I fear you have been lied to.'

'What did you mean by your comment about Leonard trying to kill you, again? Are you daring to assert that my son tried to dispatch of you?'

'I do not make this accusation on a whim, my lord,' said Bronwyn.

'You have no proof of this appalling slur!' Price spat.

Bronwyn glared at Price. 'Proof? Is my standing here when you told every soul I know that I was dead not a good place to start?'

'That proves nothing,' Price sneered.

'Enough,' said the Earl. 'Ms Rees, I will hear your tale. Though I yet reserve judgement on my son.'

Bronwyn nodded. 'My lord, I thought your son an honourable man, but in my time at sea I have heard about his most gravely shameful behaviour. I suspect that is in part why he sank the ship I was, until that point, travelling safely on.'

'I know he sunk your ship,' the Earl said. 'I sent Mr Medlyn with all the treasure those barbarian pirates requested to bring you home, including my late wife's most treasured jewel, The Eye of the Sun. Despite my offering these jewels in good faith when Mr Medlyn returned, he reported that the pirates stole the treasure and refused to hand you back, and that's why he sunk the ship.'

'I regret to inform you that is not the truth, my lord,' said Bronwyn.

'My lord, if I may–' Medlyn began.

'No you may not!' The Earl shouted. 'I am talking to Miss Rees and nobody else.'

'No treasure was taken by those pirates, Sir,' Bronwyn clarified. 'Medlyn spoke to the captain of the ship with me present. I witnessed the whole conversation. Medlyn merely boarded the vessel to inform the captain and me that my life was not worth bartering for. He then sank our ship and left us for dead.' On saying those words out loud, Bronwyn turned on Price and Medlyn. 'If Mr Price wants proof, I'd wager that a thorough search of his quarters will provide you with all of the proof you need. For if I was to guess as to the whereabouts of your treasure, including your dear wife's precious jewel, my lord, I would have to say it was still in the possession of your son. I didn't know until this moment, but he not only tried to have me killed, he used my kidnap to extort riches from you.'

Bronwyn could hear the fury in her voice. She could remember very few times in her life when she'd had cause to be angry with anyone. She'd been angry with Miles when he kidnapped her of course, but the rage she felt now penetrated every nerve in her body.

'Why, you stupid little wench,' Price barked and slapped Bronwyn hard across the face. After everything this pitiful excuse for a man had put her through, this latest insult was the last straw. Bronwyn raised her fist to punch him but the Earl's bellow stopped her in her tracks.

'Leonard Louis Price! How dare you hit this woman?' The Earl's stare had turned only harder in his anger. 'You are a disgrace to treat a lady thus. Control yourself this instant.'

Price visibly shrank at his father's reprimand.

The Earl paused. When he spoke again his voice was quieter but just as grave. 'You have always been a disappointment, Leonard but even I didn't think you would stoop to such grave deception, until just now. If you are innocent, why would you react to the lady with such vehemence? Your quarters will be thoroughly searched, of that you can be sure. And if the jewels are found, well then may God Almighty help you.'

'Father...' Price began but the Earl held up a hand to silence him.

'If those jewels are found in your possession, you'll get not another gold coin from me as long as I live.'

'But father, I really don't know –' Price started to blabber but one look at his father's face and he said not one more word.

The Earl strode towards Bronwyn and took her hands in his. 'Whatever the full truth of this matter, you have been through a terrible ordeal, my dear girl. And in the time I have known you, you have shown me nothing but kindness. Is there anything I can do to help you at this time?'

Bronwyn shook her head. 'I need nothing for myself, my lord, but I would like you to find some way of recompensing the men who brought me safely home.'

'Of course, of course, without them I would know nothing of my son's potential deception,' the Earl said. 'Are they here?

Bronwyn pushed two fingers in her mouth and whistled hard through her teeth.

A moment later, the doors at the back of the cathedral opened. Rookwood and Jimmy walked in followed by Miles, Gwenllian and Dodger. Dodger tried to make a run for Bronwyn the moment he saw her, but Gwenllian grabbed hold of him.

On seeing Miles, Bronwyn's heart caught in her throat. They had known that the Earl would not pay anything to men dressed as pirates, so Rookwood had agreed to use the last of his money to buy them new clothes for the task. Miles wore a white linen shirt, a waistcoat embroidered in gold, a black overcoat made of the finest cotton and breeches to match. His long, sandy hair was tied back with a black ribbon. He almost looked like a gentleman.

Miles strode towards the altar. It took a moment for Price to recognise him but the whole cathedral knew about it when he did.

'That's the pirate who stole her away in the first place!' Price shouted. 'They're in on it together to ruin me.'

'My lord,' Miles greeted the Earl, ignoring Price completely.

'Young man,' The Earl said. His stare steely and cold. 'The last I saw of you, you shouted terrible slanders at my son and stole his bride away, threatening to kill her no less.'

Miles dipped his head in shame. 'I can only apologise for the harm caused to you, my lord. But I beg you to hear my full explanation. If after hearing the full truth of the matter you wish to have me imprisoned or... worse, I shall not resist my sentence. I am at your mercy.'

Bronwyn swallowed hard, her eyes widening at her beloved's words. She hadn't known Miles was going to make any such bargain. That hadn't been part of the plan.

The Earl's stare did not soften but he offered a nod of agreement. 'Very well, what have you to say?'

'My name is Miles Nash, my lord. I come from New York. You may remember your son's first wife, Cecily?'

The Earl eyed Miles harder over his spectacles. 'Of course I remember, what of her?'

'I was a dear friend of Cecily's, and it grieves me to tell you that she took her life due to the negligence of your son.'

'My son had told me the girl had always been in quiet misery and had talked about ending her life for some time,' the Earl said.

Miles shook his head. 'When I first came to know her she was the very picture of youth and happiness. But your son spent her fortune and left her in such a position that she could not even buy bread.'

The Earl's stare darted at Price for a moment, but then fixed once again on Miles.

'And I'm afraid that is not the worst of it, my lord. It pains me to tell you the rest, but I fear I must,' said Miles. 'Before she died, she confided in me that she was with child. She was carrying your grandchild but could not face another day after your son left her scrabbling for food. It was for these wrongs that I kidnapped Bronwyn, to spite your son. I thought it was the way to avenge Cecily's death. But Bronwyn showed me I was wrong. She has led me back to the light. I am a changed man, my lord. Please believe me that your son has done a great disservice to his title and his family name.'

The Earl took a moment to digest all that Miles had to say before turning to his son, his eyes watery and full of confusion. 'Cecily was carrying a child?'

Leonard looked anywhere but at his father.

'Answer me!'

'Yes, but who knows if the child was mine? It was probably his!' Leonard jabbed an accusing finger in Miles's direction and Bronwyn held her breath. She wasn't sure if Miles would allow him to say those words and live. As much as she thought Price deserved to die for all he'd done, she had seen the look on Miles's face when he'd killed Roberts back in La Rochelle. His very soul was in agony. She didn't wish him to go through that again for a worm like Leonard Price.

Miles took three deliberate steps towards the Viscount. He towered over him. There was no question about who would win in a fair fight. 'How dare you question the loyalty of a woman as faithful as Cecily,' Miles growled. 'The child was not mine but I would have cared for it like it was if she had lived. Which is more than can be said for you.'

'I have heard enough,' said the Earl. 'I am sickened by my own flesh and blood. Step away from him, Mr Nash. I will deal with this poor excuse for a son myself. And, as requested by Miss Rees, should our family treasures be found in my son's quarters, you and your companions will be compensated as I see fit.'

Miles turned back to the Earl and shook his head. 'I need no recompense, my lord. I just ask that, if the treasure is recovered as I believe it will be, you reward my faithful companions who have helped me bring this lady home.' Miles shot Jimmy and Rookwood a measured smile. 'I will earn my own way.'

The Earl nodded. It seemed their plan had worked.

Bronwyn sighed in relief and turned to Miles.

'Look at you,' she said to him. 'I almost didn't recognise the man I love.'

Miles opened his mouth to reply but before he could Bronwyn heard Gwenllian scream. 'Look out!'

In the same instant, a tortured expression crossed Miles's face and he fell to his knees. Behind him, Leonard Price stood with a bloody knife in his hands and a self-satisfied leer on his lips.

Barely able to believe what she was seeing, Bronwyn dropped to the floor and cradled Miles's head in her arms. 'Somebody fetch the doctor,' she half-screamed through her tears. 'Hurry, hurry, please!'

Bronwyn could hear some of the men in the congregation rushing to restrain Price from further attack and dragging him away. He was hurling all manner of abuse while Dodger yipped and barked and howled. But despite the numerous distractions, all Bronwyn could focus on was the light in those amber eyes.

'Miles, please, please don't die,' Bronwyn whispered as she watched those eyes flutter closed.

CHAPTER TWENTY SIX

The first thing Miles sensed was the scent of ripe grapefruit. That was what told him he was home. In truth he had no idea where he was at all. He only knew that Bronwyn was near and as far as he was concerned, she was his home now.

'Easy there,' he heard her soft voice say before a cold, wet cloth to the forehead granted him some relief.

Slowly, he prised open his eyes just enough so he could look at her. She was wearing a corseted dress in dark blue which he would have loved to tear off her if only he had the strength to lift his arms.

'Bronwyn,' he croaked, and a moment later she held a mug of water to his mouth. He gulped down the cool liquid and when he had finished, she planted a soft kiss on his lips.

'I think talking is a bit ambitious right now, so why don't you just lay there like a lifeless lump instead?' She paused for just a moment before adding. 'Oh, that's very good. Keep practicing and you'll be the best lifeless lump in the village by the end of the week, though I must warn you, you've some stiff competition on that score.'

If he could have laughed, he would have. Instead he managed a smile, or something that looked enough like one that she smiled in return.

'Price?'

'Well of course, while you've been barely awake for the past ten days you've missed all of the action. The Earl had Price's quarters and Medlyn's too. Between them they'd hidden all the treasure the Earl had given them for my release. As far as the Earl was concerned, this was proof enough that we were the ones telling the truth, not his son.'

'What...' Miles forced himself to speak again. 'What will become of him?'

'Oh, you know how it is in this country, titled people don't hang as often as they might unless it's for treason, but the Earl insisted his son be put behind bars, stating he was a danger to others.'

'He's in prison?'

'Yes, and from the way the Earl was speaking, I doubt he's going to be out for a very long time. The Earl has sent several letters asking after your health. Graciously, he kept your former indiscretions out of it when he explained to the judge what his son had been up to.'

Miles's eyes filled with tears. 'So Price didn't hurt you?'

'No, my love, he didn't,' Bronwyn took his hand in hers and kissed it. 'But I came very close to hurting him. The Earl himself looked half-tempted to let me make my mark on him.'

'I thought he was going to hurt you. I thought he was going to kill you.'

'Well, I would have been very lonely in heaven if he had, wouldn't I? You didn't die. Which I'm rather glad about, it has to be said.'

Miles rested his voice, hoping the glowing feeling in his chest somehow reached his eyes so she would know what a balm her good humour was to his wounds. It hurt to talk but there was so much he wanted to say to her. He took a moment to look around the room. By the wooden beams he guessed he must be in a bedroom at the cottage. The mattress felt so soft after his years of sleeping in make-shift cots at sea. Could this really be his life now? Living here, in comfort, with this woman?

Miles cleared his throat and spoke as softly as he could, so as not to strain his voice. 'When Price stabbed me, and I fell to the ground, I couldn't speak because I was in so much pain.'

The gentle smile fell from Bronwyn's face. 'I've never been so terrified.'

'Neither have I,' he paused briefly, summoning the strength to speak further. 'Not because I thought I was going to die. I've thought that many times over the last five years and you were with me for several of them. I was terrified of dying without having at least had the chance to ask you to marry me. To watch your reaction as I asked you, and find out your answer.'

Bronwyn's breath hitched at his words and her eyes widened.

'I had planned to take you for an intimate picnic, somewhere secluded,' he said, his eyes flashing with desire. 'I had already begun thinking about the promises I would make to you. How I would always protect you. How I would put your needs first. How I would love you with more passion than any other man ever could. But I think, even after this short time, you already know all this about me. And it seems we cannot stay out of trouble for more than a day. So before someone else bludgeons me into the ocean, stabs me in the back or otherwise tries to prevent me from seeing another sunrise, I need to ask you, urgently: Bronwyn, will you be my wife?'

Privately, Miles berated himself for not being able to wait for a more appropriate juncture to ask her this question. She deserved the scene he had described. The intimate picnic. The doting suitor at full strength to make his passions known. But he had spent the last ten days drifting between life and death, and he believed that a need to know the answer to this question is what had coaxed him back to the world of the living. He could not bear to delay another instant no matter how improper it may seem.

She paused for a moment and stared into his eyes. Then she leaned over him brushed the hair out of his face and kissed him first on the forehead. Then on the nose and then hovered her lips over his. 'Do I get Dodger into the bargain?'

Miles let out a small sigh. 'I don't think that useless mutt will be easily parted from you as long as he lives and breathes.'

'Then, yes, I will marry you on one very important condition.'

The lightness of her tone indicated this was another one of her little rouses but just in case, Miles responded solemnly. 'Name it.'

'That even though you'll likely be land-locked for the rest of your days, I can still refer to you as my captain.'

Miles chuckled, and then groaned at the stabbing pain in his back. 'I think I can live with that,' he returned.

'Then let us be married, my captain, and I will see if I can make an honourable gentleman out of you.'

'How about an honourable rogue?'

'How about a gentleman pirate?' Bronwyn said with a smile.

Staring into those tempestuous blue eyes, he mustered the strength to graze her cheek with the back of his hand. He thought about all the future days he would spend kissing those precious scars on her face, chuckling at the unexpectedly brazen words that so often fell from those sumptuous lips, and cradling her as she fell to sleep knowing that while he was present she would be shielded from harm, always. Looking at her now, he realised that every man, pirate or no, needed a horizon to sail towards.

And she was his.

If you would like to receive my next book before anyone else and at a discounted price, please sign-up to my romance mailing list at: helencoxbooks.com/mailinglist

If you enjoyed this work, please take the time to leave a review. ♥

You may also enjoy these other titles by Helen Louise Cox:
Disarming the Wildest Warrior
Once Upon a Rugged Knight
Swept Away by the Merman

CHAPTER TWENTY SIX

ACKNOWLEDGEMENTS

A huge thank you to my editor Ann Leanders for all her time spent shaping this story into a publishable manuscript. Thanks are also due to my designer, Hammad Khalid for his ongoing work on turning my stories into books of publishable standard. I could not ask for a more dedicated and talented team.

Thank you also to my husband Jo who is in the unfortunate predicament of being a historian married to a historical romance writer. Does he get any peace from my endless research questions? Very little. A gold star for him.

ABOUT THE AUTHOR

Helen Louise Cox is a Yorkshire-born novelist and poet. After completing her MA in creative writing at the University of York St. John Helen wrote for a range of publications, edited her own independent film magazine for five years and penned three non-fiction books. Her first two novels were published by HarperCollins in 2016. She currently lives by the sea in Sunderland where she writes poetry, romance novellas, and The Kitt Hartley series alongside hosting The Poetrygram podcast.

https://helencoxbooks.com

Printed in Great Britain
by Amazon